Go ahead and scream.

No one can hear you. You're no longer in the safe world you know.

You've taken a terrifying step . . .

into the darkest corners of your imagination.

You've opened the door to . . .

Read all the books in

the NiGHtmare Room

series by R.L. Stine

Full Moon Halloween

R.L. STINE

AVON BOOKS
An Imprint of HarperCollinsPublishers

PARACHUTE PRESS

Full Moon Halloween

Printed in the United States of America.

For information address:
HarperCollins Children's Books,
a division of HarperCollins Publishers,
1350 Avenue of the Americas,
New York, NY 10019.

Library of Congress Catalog Card Number: 2001117191
ISBN 0-06-440908-2

First Avon edition, 2001

AVON TRADEMARK REG. U.S. PAT. OFF. AND IN OTHER
COUNTRIES, MARCA REGISTRADA, HECHO EN U.S.A.

Visit us on the World Wide Web!
www.harperchildrens.com

Welcome . . .

Hello, I'm R.L. Stine. Picture a clear, cool October night. Then picture a bright full moon glowing high in the purple-black night sky.

Do you see a boy and girl hurrying down the street? That's Tristan and his friend Rosa. They are on their way to a Halloween party.

They are also on their way to the most frightening night of their lives.

You see, terrifying things happen when the moon is full on Halloween night. Especially when your Halloween party is being held in . . . *THE NIGHTMARE ROOM*.

the NiGHtmare Room

Full Moon Halloween

"Hey—wait up!"

Tristan Gottschalk hurried to catch up to his friends. His shoes thudded against the hard floor. The sound echoed down the long, empty hall.

He wrapped his arm around Ray Davidoff's neck and tightened it into a choke hold. "Come on! WWF Smackdown!"

Ray jerked free of Tristan's hold. "You don't have the guts to challenge Stone Cold Ray!" he bellowed. He grabbed Tristan's arm in an armlock and shoved it up behind Tristan's back until he screamed.

Wrestling playfully, the two boys slammed into the metal lockers along the wall.

Rosa Martinez pulled Ray off Tristan. "Grow up,"

she said. "Let's just get out of here."

Bella Chester agreed. "The school is so creepy when everyone is gone. I can't believe we missed the late bus."

"It's dark out already," Rosa said. "And why do they dim the lights in this school so early?"

Ray laughed. "Big Bad Rosa. Since when are you afraid of the dark?"

Rosa gave him a hard shove. "I *told* you not to call me that. I'm tall—I'm not big!"

"You're bigger than *me!*" Ray cried.

Rosa scowled at him. "Can I help it if you're a shrimp?"

Tristan laughed. "You're calling Stone Cold Ray a shrimp? Just because my dog is taller than he is?"

"Hey!" Ray frowned at them both. "I had a growth spurt last month. Dad says I could grow another six inches this year."

"Why are we talking about this?" Bella asked. "Hear how our voices carry down the hall? Everyone can hear our stupid conversation."

"But there's no one here," Rosa said. "The school is empty. Everyone has gone home."

"Love the echo," Ray said. He tossed back his head and let out a long, high animal howl.

Tristan laughed. "The cry of the wolf!" He joined in and they howled together.

"Give us a break," Bella groaned. She swept back

her long, curly red hair. "That's not funny. Don't you watch the news on TV? Haven't you heard about the animal attacks?"

Ray sneered. "You mean you believe that junk about werewolves prowling the town? Those are just rumors. A bunch of really bored people probably made it up."

"But did you see the two cats that were attacked?" Bella replied. "They were torn apart and eaten. There was nothing left of them but their heads. Two cat heads lying in the dirt with big paw-prints all around."

"Yuck," Rosa said, making a face. "Shut up about that."

"Yeah. You're making me hungry!" Ray exclaimed.

He and Tristan cupped their hands around their mouths and howled again.

"I can't believe Mr. Moon kept us after school so long," Rosa said, ignoring them.

"Yeah. Why did he ask *us* to help out with his science experiments?" Bella asked. "We're not the brains in the class."

"Maybe he likes us," Rosa said.

"Ha-ha," Ray replied sarcastically. "You're kidding—right?"

They stopped at their lockers. Bella dropped some books onto her locker floor. Then she pulled out her black fleece jacket.

"I hate Mr. Moon's smile," she said. "It's like he has five hundred teeth."

"Mr. Moon looks like a vampire in an old movie," Rosa said. She pulled a red wool cap down over her short black hair. "With his hair slicked straight back like that. And those heavy eyebrows. And those beady, round eyes."

Tristan glanced down the hall. "Quiet. He can probably hear every word we're saying."

"No way," Ray said. "I'll bet you he's still in the lab, injecting weird things into bird eggs."

"I think those experiments are kind of cool," Tristan said. He hiked his backpack over the shoulders of his jean jacket. "I mean, I like the idea of putting strange things in eggs and then seeing what you get."

"Don't ever invite me to your house for breakfast!" Rosa exclaimed.

They all laughed.

Rosa always cracked them up.

Ray slapped Rosa a high-five.

They slammed their lockers shut and locked them. Then they made their way through the dimly lit hall to the back exit of the school.

The four of us have been friends for a long time, Tristan thought. But Mr. Moon doesn't know that. We're not even in the same science class.

So why did he pick us to help with his experiments today?

They passed an orange-and-black poster about a school Halloween party.

"Wow. Almost Halloween," Rosa said. "Are we trick-or-treating this year?"

Bella twisted her face, thinking hard. Whenever she did this, her green cat eyes seemed to disappear into her freckles. "I don't know," she replied. "Are we too old? How old is *too* old to trick-or-treat?"

"I think twelve is too old," Tristan replied. "And we're all twelve."

"Who cares?" Ray said. "We still want candy—right? So, that means we're *not* too old. We should go out."

He bumped Bella against the wall. "Unless you're afraid of the werewolves!"

"I'm not afraid of the werewolves," Bella said, bumping him back. "But if we go out, it means we need costumes."

"Why don't we have a party this year?" Ray asked. "A costume party would be awesome. I'll put tattoos all over my chest and arms and come as Stone Cold Ray."

He let out a deafening cheer and wrapped Tristan in a headlock. "You got a problem with that? You got a problem with that?" he barked.

It was his favorite wrestling line. He drove them crazy repeating it all the time. "You got a problem with that?"

Tristan wrestled free. "Yeah, I've got a problem with that," he said.

He smoothed down his wavy straw-colored hair. "If we have a party, there won't be time to trick-or-treat."

They were nearly to the door. Through the window, Tristan could see a ghostly pale moon—shimmery and round—still low in the late afternoon sky.

As they started to leave the school building, he glanced back—and gasped when he saw someone behind them.

Someone standing very still against the dark wall, watching them, listening to them.

"Hey—" Tristan muttered to the others. All four of them turned around.

Squinting in the dim light, Tristan recognized the kid. A guy from their class.

Michael Moon, the teacher's son.

A strange kid. Skinny and dark with Mr. Moon's slicked-back black hair, tiny round eyes, and a narrow, unpleasant face.

A face like a ferret, Tristan thought.

Michael Moon, who kept to himself and barely ever spoke. Who didn't seem to have any friends in school.

Leaning against the wall, Michael watched Tristan and his friends with his hands stuffed into the pockets of his black jeans.

And then suddenly he straightened.

He raised his hands to his mouth. And he called out two words to them.

Just two words in his high, whispery voice.

Two words that sent a chill down Tristan's back.

"Be careful."

A few minutes later Rosa followed Tristan into his house. "That kid gives me the creeps," Rosa said.

Tristan stared at her. "Who? Ray?"

"No, idiot!" Laughing, she gave him a hard shove. "Michael Moon."

She pulled off her cap and glanced in the hall mirror. Using her fingers, she combed her dark hair. Then she took off her down vest and tossed it onto the bench near the door.

She wore a loose purple sweater over baggy cargo khakis. She took one last glance in the mirror, then turned back to Tristan.

"*Be careful?* So why do you think Michael Moon said that to us?" she asked.

Tristan shrugged. "Beats me. Was he warning us about something? Or was he threatening us?"

"I—I couldn't tell," Rosa replied. "But the way he said it—it really was kind of frightening."

"I guess."

Tristan dropped his backpack on the front stairs and made his way to the kitchen. "Mom? Are you home?"

"I'm in the den," his mother called. "Who are you talking to?"

"Rosa came home with me," Tristan said. He poked his head into the small den.

Mrs. Gottschalk had the news on the TV and a magazine in her lap. She always did at least two or three things at once. It was a family joke how she couldn't watch TV without reading and talking on the phone at the same time.

Tristan looked a lot like his mother. Both were tall and thin. He had her curly straw-colored hair. And her round blue eyes and short stubby nose.

She raised the remote and muted the TV sound. "Hi, Rosa. How come you two are so late?"

"Mr. Moon asked us to help with some science experiments," Tristan answered.

"They were kind of interesting," Rosa added. "So we lost track of the time."

"Mr. Moon—isn't that the new teacher?" his mom said. "I haven't met him yet."

"He's okay," Rosa said. "A little strange."

Mrs. Gottschalk raised an eyebrow. "Strange?"

"Yeah, but it's no big deal," Tristan said. "We're starving. Is there anything we can eat?"

His mother frowned at him. "It's almost dinnertime. Rosa, can you stay for dinner?"

"No. I have to get home," Rosa replied. "My aunt and uncle are visiting from California, and I have to baby-sit my little cousin."

Tristan made his way to the kitchen to look for a snack. Rosa followed close behind. "My cousin Benny is an animal," she said. "He's four years old, and he still bites."

Tristan reached into a cabinet for a bag of chocolate chip cookies. "Really? What do you do when he bites you?"

"I bite him back!" Rosa replied.

They both laughed.

Tristan handed Rosa a couple of cookies. Then, he popped a whole one into his own mouth.

Chewing noisily, he began to paw through the stack of mail on the kitchen counter.

He pulled out a square black envelope. The name and address were printed in orange ink. "Hey—this is for me," he said.

Rosa examined the envelope. "Black and orange? It looks like a Halloween party invitation."

"Weird," Tristan said. "We don't know anyone

who's having a party, do we?"

He tore off the top of the envelope.

The envelope exploded with a loud *pop*.

Startled, Tristan dropped it to the counter.

And let out a scream as thick black smoke came shooting out.

Tristan's heart pounded as he watched the black smoke curl up from the torn envelope. After a few seconds, it faded away.

Rosa laughed. "Whoa. Someone really wants to get your attention!"

Tristan's mom came running into the kitchen. "What was that explosion? What happened? I smell smoke!" Her eyes were wide with panic.

"Just a trick envelope," Tristan said. He picked it up carefully.

Would it explode again?

No. He pulled out a black-and-orange card. *"Come to the scariest Halloween party ever!"* he read. "You were right, Rosa. It's a party invitation."

"Who sent it?" Rosa asked.

Tristan gazed down to the bottom of the card. "I don't believe this. It's from Mr. Moon."

"You're kidding!" Rosa exclaimed.

"Let me see that," Tristan's mom said. She took the card from him and read it carefully. "Well, isn't that nice? Your teacher is having a Halloween party."

"Nice?" Tristan asked weakly. "What's nice about it?"

"It's horrible," Rosa groaned. "We don't want to spend Halloween with a teacher. We want to have fun and hang out with our friends."

"He's a new teacher," Mrs. Gottschalk said. "He wants to get to know you kids."

Rosa groaned. "I wonder if I got invited, too."

She picked up the phone and punched in her number. "Mom, hi. It's me. . . . Yeah, I'm at Tristan's. Did I get a black envelope in the mail?"

Rosa groaned again. "I did? Oh. No—don't open it. Mom, really. Don't open it. I'll be home in a few minutes." She clicked off the phone.

"Mr. Moon probably invited *all* of his students," Tristan's mom said. "So it'll be fun."

"Thrills and chills," Tristan said, rolling his eyes.

Rosa shook her head sadly. "Halloween with a teacher," she said. "This is *so* not fair. And it's our last year to trick-or-treat."

"We'll probably sit around drinking apple juice

and telling really dumb ghost stories," Tristan said, sighing. "Bor-ring."

"And we'll play some babyish games," Rosa said. "You know. Pin the Tail on the Pumpkin or something."

Tristan laughed. She always made him laugh.

"You don't have to stay the whole time," his mother said.

Tristan turned to her. "Huh? What do you mean?"

"Just stay for a little while. Stay for an hour. You know. To be polite. Then go trick-or-treating with your friends."

"Cool!" Tristan said.

"Totally cool," Rosa agreed. "But do you think it'll be easy to leave the party?"

"It shouldn't be a problem," Tristan's mom replied. "Why would it be a problem?"

Across town, Mr. Moon and his wife, Angela, were preparing their house for the Halloween party.

Mr. Moon wore baggy khakis and a maroon sweatshirt torn at the neck.

His wife was a large woman, with a round pink face surrounded by frizzy blond hair that stuck out in all directions. She wore thick square-shaped glasses that made her gray eyes look as big as silver dollars.

"This is a shabby old house," Angela said, stretching a streamer of black crepe paper across the living room wall. "What a shame we haven't had time to fix it up."

A thin smile spread over Mr. Moon's face. "It's perfect for our party," he said. "It's cold and drafty. The wallpaper is torn. The rugs are stained. Very creepy."

"I think our next house should be brand new," Angela replied. "And I think we should paint the walls white and yellow. I'd like to live in a bright, shiny house."

"Maybe," Mr. Moon muttered. He was arranging plastic skulls in a row on the mantelpiece.

"I agree with Mom," Michael Moon said, stepping into the room. He wore a black T-shirt with a photo of Jimi Hendrix over the front, pulled down over black jeans.

He was chewing an apple, turning it as if he were eating an ear of corn. Juice ran down his narrow, pointed chin.

"I'm tired of living in these creepy old barns," he said.

Mr. Moon's heavy black eyebrows shot up. "Did we ask for your opinion?" he snapped.

"Why do we have to have this party?" Michael asked.

"You'll have fun," his mother replied. "You know our parties are always exciting. And you'll get to spend time with your new friends."

"I don't have any new friends," Michael said,

scowling. "How can I make friends when I have to change schools every year?"

"Help your mom with the crepe paper," Mr. Moon ordered.

"Listen to me," Michael insisted. "Don't have this party. Please. I'm begging you."

Angela turned and studied him. "Michael, you know we *have* to have the Halloween party. We *always* have the party, don't we?"

Mr. Moon stepped between them. "Michael, stop arguing," he said sternly. "This is going to be the best party yet. Put on your coat and run down to the corner. We need more black streamers."

"Buy as many as you can," Angela said.

"But—why won't you listen to me?" Michael whined.

"Buy more orange streamers, too," Angela said. "This party has to be special."

Grumbling to himself, Michael grabbed his coat from the closet. Then he stomped angrily out of the house, slamming the front door behind him.

"He used to be fun," Mr. Moon said, shaking his head. "When he was little, we always had a good time together. But now . . ."

"He's just going through a phase," Angela said.

"I hope so." Mr. Moon sighed. He swept a hand back through his straight black hair. "Let's check the windows," he said. "Try the control."

Angela moved to the bookshelves on the back wall. She lifted away a stack of books.

She pulled out a square black metal box and opened it with a key. Inside were three red buttons. Angela pushed the top button.

Clang. Clang clang. Clang.

They both watched as steel bars slammed down over all of the windows.

Smiling, Mr. Moon walked over to the front window. He wrapped his hands around two of the bars and tugged.

"Solid," he said. "Very good."

"I tested the doors," Angela told him. "They all lock automatically when I push the middle button."

"Excellent," Mr. Moon said, his smile growing wider. "Excellent. Doors locked. Windows barred. That will keep them in. I don't want any of these kids to escape."

The next morning, Tristan made his way down the aisle of the school bus to his usual seat in the back row.

"Hey, Tristan—"

"Yo—what's up?"

"How ya doin'?"

Tristan slapped hands as he walked to the back. He was one of the most popular kids at Wordsworth Middle School. He had a lot of friends because he was smart and funny, quiet, and easy to get along with.

The next stop was in front of Ray's house. Ray came running down the driveway, struggling into his jacket. Late as usual.

"Stone Cold Ray is in the house!" he shouted, climbing aboard.

"Give me a break," the bus driver muttered.

"Hey, Ray—stand up!" a kid shouted from the aisle.

Lots of kids laughed. Everyone knew Ray hated being so short.

"You got a problem with that? You got a problem with that?" Ray shook his fists and acted tough as he made his way to the back.

"Hey!" Ray cried out as someone bounced a milk carton off his head.

More laughter.

"You got a problem with that?" Ray screamed. "Anybody want a piece of me? You want a piece of me?"

"Everybody settle down," the driver shouted, turning in his seat. "That means you, Stone Cold. Or you can be stone cold outside as you walk to school!"

Ray dropped into the space between Tristan and Rosa. "Look at them shaking," he said. "I've got them all scared."

Rosa shook her head. "They don't know you're joking. One of these days you're going to get pounded."

Ray stared at her. "Joking?"

"Hey, Ray—did you get a party invitation in the mail yesterday—from Mr. Moon?" Tristan asked. He was eager to change the subject.

Ray nodded. "Yeah. It blew up in my face. Pretty cool."

Bella's house was the last stop on the bus route. She climbed on and waved to them as she dropped into the last empty seat near the front.

"We're not going to Moon's party, are we?" Ray asked.

"I don't want to," Tristan answered. "But my mom says I have to."

"We won't stay long," Rosa added. "Maybe just an hour."

Ray made a face. "Hey, Kimball!" he called to a kid near the front. "Did you get Moon's party invitation yesterday?"

"Huh? From Michael Moon?" the kid asked. "Is he having a party?"

"No—from his father," Ray answered.

"Is it a costume party?" another boy shouted. "Is Michael going to come as a human?"

A few kids laughed.

"I didn't get any invitation," Kimball said.

"Did *anybody* get an invitation to Moon's party?" Ray shouted.

Silence. A lot of kids shook their heads *no*.

Only one hand went up. "I got one," Bella called.

"Weird," Rosa murmured. "Just the four of us? Are we the only ones invited to the party?"

● ● ●

Later, in the lunchroom, they asked more kids if they'd received invitations.

But no one they asked had gotten one. No one seemed to know that Mr. Moon was having a Halloween party.

"Weird. Totally weird," Bella said, finishing her fried chicken. She took a long sip from her orange juice carton.

"Yes, you *are* weird," Ray said, staring at Bella's lunch plate. "Do you always eat the chicken bones, too?"

"I don't eat them. I just chew on them," Bella replied. She raised two fists. "*You* got a problem with that?"

Rosa stared at Bella's gnawed chicken bones. "That's gross," she said. "My dog eats bones. But I really don't know any people who eat—"

"OWOOOOOOOOO!" Ray tossed back his head and let out a long wolf-howl. "I eat bones!" Ray snapped his teeth at Rosa. "Stone Cold Ray eats *human* bones! OWWOOOOOOOO!"

Rosa shoved him so hard, he nearly fell off his chair.

"Time to go," Tristan said, climbing to his feet. "Before we get *thrown* out."

The four of them made their way out to the hall.

Tristan glanced up and down the hall to make sure Mr. Moon wasn't nearby. "Do you realize we haven't found anyone else who has been invited to Moon's party?" he asked.

"We can't be the only ones—can we?" Rosa said.

"I'll bet he invited a bunch of kids from his old school," Bella said.

Ray pounded lockers with his fist as he followed them down the long hall. "Yeah. You're right. Probably a bunch of kids we don't know."

Tristan turned—and once again saw someone watching them.

Michael Moon. Huddled in a classroom doorway. Half-hidden from view.

Is he following us? Tristan wondered.

What does he want? Why is he watching us like that? What's going on?

"Some of you may wonder about my name," Mr. Moon said. He carried a long pointer and paced back and forth in front of his desk.

Tristan sat next to Ray in the front row of the classroom. Sunlight washed over them from the window. Heat coming up from the radiator against the wall made it rattle.

Mr. Moon wore a loose red sweater over baggy gray pants. When he stepped into the sunlight, his pale face appeared to glow.

"Some of you may already know that there will be a full moon this Halloween," he said. He tapped the desktop with the end of the pointer.

Why does he keep staring at Ray and me? Tristan wondered.

He paces back and forth. But every time he turns our way, he keeps his eyes on the two of us.

What is his problem?

"*Luna* means moon," the teacher continued. "Can you think of words that come from *luna*?"

"Looney Tunes?" Ray called out.

Kids laughed.

"It isn't funny. Ray is right," Mr. Moon said, nodding at Ray.

The laughter stopped instantly.

Ray flashed Tristan a thumbs-up. "Tell the truth. Am I a genius, or what?"

"The words *lunacy* and *lunatic* come from *luna*," the teacher continued, ignoring Ray.

"So that means we should call him *Mr. Lunatic*," Ray whispered to Tristan.

Tristan struggled not to burst out laughing.

"Something funny?" Mr. Moon asked. He leaned over Tristan, the pointer raised.

"Not really," Tristan replied. "Just Ray's face."

That got a big laugh from everyone but Ray.

"Let's try to keep on the subject," Mr. Moon said softly. He kept his gaze on Tristan. "We were talking about the word *lunatic*."

He cleared his throat and narrowed his eyes at Tristan. "People who howled at the moon were called *lunatics*. As the years passed by, lots of other legends grew about the full moon."

He turned to the rest of the class. "Do you know any legends about the full moon?"

A girl named Kim-Lee raised her hand.

"Don't they say that more crimes happen on the nights of the full moon?" she asked. "You know. Robberies and murders and everything?"

Mr. Moon nodded. "Yes. Police report that their busiest nights are full-moon nights. Many more crimes are committed. Any others?"

Silence.

Then Kim-Lee raised her hand again. "And doesn't the moon control the ocean waves?"

"Well, the pull of the moon is said to affect the ocean tides," Mr. Moon replied.

Tristan raised his hand. "What about were-wolves?" he asked. "Some people think that were-wolves come out when the full moon is at its highest, right?"

"Yes." Mr. Moon shook his head and *tsk-tsk*ed.

"I'm sure that all of you have seen the frightening reports on the news about the recent animal attacks," he said. "Some people are blaming the attacks on werewolves."

He paused.

"Werewolf attacks. Right here in our town. It's hard to believe. Do werewolves exist or not?" he muttered. "Perhaps we'll find out during the full moon on Halloween night."

Suddenly Ray jumped to his feet. His eyes bulged in horror.

"My hands!" he screamed. "Oh, no! My hands! They're growing fur!"

On Halloween, a few nights later, Tristan found himself thinking about Ray's dumb werewolf joke in class.

Why did Mr. Moon get so upset? Tristan wondered. The teacher totally freaked. He turned bright red and gaped at Ray, shaking in fright.

Didn't Moon know that Ray was just being Ray? Couldn't he tell it was a joke?

Tristan pulled the wide-brimmed hat down over his hair. Gazing into the mirror, he adjusted the black mask that covered his eyes.

"Tristan, where did you find that stuff?" His mom stepped up behind him, shaking her head.

"It was all in my old toy chest," he replied. He pulled a cap pistol from the holster at his waist and twirled it on his finger. "Wish I still had some caps."

"Do kids these days know what a cowboy is?" Mrs. Gottschalk asked.

Tristan tugged at the mask. It made his face itch. "Not really," he said. "No one is into cowboys. That's why I like the costume."

His mom straightened the white cowboy hat. "This is a little small. It will blow off in the wind."

"We're going to be indoors—remember?" Tristan replied with a groan. "We're going to be at that stupid party."

"Maybe it will be fun," she said. "If your whole class comes . . ."

"My whole class *isn't* coming," Tristan replied, tying a red bandanna around his neck. "We asked a whole bunch of kids at school if they were coming. No one even heard of this party. He must be inviting kids we don't know."

"Let me tie that for you. You're messing it up." She leaned down and began to knot the bandanna. "Are you supposed to be the Lone Ranger?"

"Who's that?" Tristan asked.

He gazed out the bedroom window. A silvery full moon was rising over the treetops. Thin wisps of cloud wriggled across the big moon like shadowy snakes.

"Where are you? Are you upstairs?" Rosa's voice

rang out from the first floor.

Tristan heard her footsteps on the stairs. He pulled both pistols as she stepped into the room. "Stick 'em up!"

Rosa's mouth dropped open. She stared wide-eyed at him for a moment. "That's the geekiest costume I ever saw," she said.

"Hey, give me a break," Tristan replied. He slid the pistols back into their leather holsters. "I'm going to be the only cowboy in town tonight."

"You've got *that* right," Rosa said, rolling her eyes.

Mrs. Gottschalk studied Rosa. "What are *you* supposed to be? A fish?"

"No way. I'm a mermaid," Rosa replied. She wore a blond wig tied high on her head in a bun. Her cheeks and forehead glittered with sparkly stuff.

"See? I drew fish scales all over this green jumpsuit with a Magic Marker," Rosa said. "I'm half fish, half girl."

"Which half is the fish half?" Tristan joked.

"Ha-ha." Rosa shoved him into the dresser.

His cowboy hat toppled off and sailed to the floor. He bent to pick it up. "Rosa, if you're a mermaid, where are your tail fins?"

"I didn't know how to make fins," she replied. "Besides, how can you walk with a tail over your feet?"

"I think she looks very . . . different," Tristan's

mom said. She glanced at the clock. "If you don't get going, you two are going to be late."

They both groaned.

"I guess you're not looking forward to Mr. Moon's party, either?" Tristan's mom asked Rosa.

Rosa shook her head. "No way."

"Well, just stay for an hour," Mrs. Gottschalk said. "Then tell Mr. Moon your parents don't want you to stay out late."

She straightened Tristan's bandanna. "It's the truth, after all," she said. "And don't forget. You both *do* have to be home by eleven—at the very latest."

"Right. Eleven," Tristan repeated.

"Mr. Moon will understand," his mom said. "Especially with all the frightening news stories on TV lately."

Tristan led the way out of the house. A gust of cold wind greeted him. He grabbed the hat with one hand to keep it from flying away.

Their shoes crunched over the gravel driveway. They both gazed up at the silvery full moon.

Tristan felt a chill start at his neck and tingle down his back.

He turned to Rosa. The moonlight washed over her, making her face shimmery and pale.

Again he turned his face to the moon. It gave off such cold, icy light.

Far in the distance, an animal howl rose over the rustle of the trees.

A dog howling?

Or a wolf?

"Why do I have such a bad feeling about tonight?" Tristan asked in a whisper.

They picked up Bella and Ray on the way to Mr. Moon's house.

Bella wore a long, pleated black dress and a starched white blouse with a high collar. She had sprayed her hair black with a white streak down the center.

"I'm Cruella De Vil," she announced. "So be careful. I'm totally mean tonight."

"How will we tell the difference?" Ray asked.

"Ha-ha. Be careful, Ray, or I'll smear your fake tattoos." Bella reached out to pinch his bare arm.

Ray pulled away. His arms were covered with blue and red tattoos. He wore silver tights and a bright red cape over a sleeveless silver muscle shirt.

His eyes peered out from a silky silver mask.

He shivered as a strong gust of wind fluttered his cape.

Rosa laughed. "Stone Cold Ray is going to be cold tonight in that little T-shirt!"

Ray raised his tattooed fists. "You got a problem with that?" he growled. "You got a problem with that?"

The wind sent Tristan's cowboy hat sailing over the grass. He chased after it. "I think there used to be a string on this thing you could tie under your chin," he said. He jammed the small hat back on his head.

"Look at those kids." Ray pointed to a group of nine or ten trick-or-treaters hurrying up a driveway across the street. "They're having fun. They don't have to go to a dumb teacher's party."

"We don't have to stay for long," Tristan said.

He heard a loud *crack* behind him. A twig breaking?

He spun around—and saw a dark figure standing half-hidden by a tall hedge.

A vampire.

White face. Dark red lips. Black hair slicked back. Long black cape fluttering in the wind.

"*Be careful,*" the vampire called softly. So softly Tristan wasn't sure he heard the words correctly.

"*Be careful.*"

"Hey—" Tristan called out to him. Was it Michael Moon?

"What's your problem?" Ray shouted.

33

Pulling the cape around him, the vampire shrank back into the darkness of the hedge.

He called out once more before he turned and started to run.

"*Don't go!*" he warned. "Don't go to that party! If you do, you won't return!"

"Hey—wait!" Tristan started to run after the vampire. But his hat sailed off his head again.

He bent to pick it up. When he stood up, the figure had vanished.

"Who was that? Was it Michael Moon?" Rosa asked. "It had to be him—right?"

"Why is he always following us?" Bella said, still squinting at the hedge.

"Because he's crazy?" Ray answered. "Because he's a total wack job?"

"You've got *that* right," Tristan said. "But for some reason, he keeps trying to warn us about something."

"Or scare us," Bella added. "Maybe it's just some kind of weird Halloween prank."

They continued walking. Ray picked up a stone and sent it bouncing down the street. Another group of trick-or-treaters came laughing and shouting out of the house on the corner.

"Why was Michael out here?" Bella asked. "Why isn't he at his dad's party?"

"Maybe he wasn't invited!" Rosa said.

They all laughed.

Bella stopped walking. "No. I know what that was about," she said. "It was part of the party. Mr. Moon sent Michael out here to scare us. He told Michael to warn us—to make the party seem really scary. It's all a joke."

"Yeah. You're right," Ray replied. "Mr. Moon is trying to make his party seem cool."

"Well, so far he's doing a lousy job." Tristan sighed. "Let's go get this over with."

A few minutes later, they stood in Mr. Moon's driveway, staring up at his house. It was a big, rambling house. Old and kind of creepy-looking.

Dark shingles. A high, slanting roof. Black shutters on the windows. A jack-o'-lantern, candlelight flickering behind its jagged grin, stared out the front window at them.

Tristan led the way as they climbed the rickety front porch. Fake cobwebs had been stretched along the wall. A large gray skull was perched on a stand near the door.

"Here goes," Tristan whispered. He raised his hand to ring the doorbell.

But the door creaked open before he had a chance to push it.

Orange light poured onto the porch. A vampire leaned his white face out. A different vampire. Taller. Older.

Mr. Moon.

"Welcome. Welcome to the House of Pain!" he declared in a low, scary voice.

He stepped back to allow them to enter. Tristan saw more thick cobwebs hanging from the ceiling. He saw black and orange streamers stretching over the living room.

"Angela, our victims have arrived!" Mr. Moon called in his movie vampire voice. He pushed back his shiny black cape, motioning for them to step farther into the hall.

"This is my wife, Angela," he said.

A large, pink-faced woman swept into the room. She wore a silky white dress that swirled out as she walked. Sparkly wings were attached to her shoulders. And a gold halo bounced on top of her piles of white-blond hair.

"Welcome! Happy Halloween!" she called. She also had a deep voice. One wing scraped against the wall as she made her way across the living room.

"Angela is an angel tonight," Mr. Moon said.

Tristan glanced into the living room. A fire danced in a wide fireplace. The lights had been turned low.

Grinning skulls had been placed around the room, along with jack-o'-lanterns with long knives stuck through their middles, and a tall cutout of a witch with her head tossed back in a cruel laugh.

Great decorations, Tristan thought. Very spooky.

He heard the front door slam hard behind him.

From somewhere past the living room, a high witch's cackle repeated over and over. The floorboards creaked as Tristan followed the others into the living room.

Tristan glanced around the room. No one else here.

No one.

He stepped up close to Rosa. He saw the frightened expression on her face.

Tristan swallowed hard. "Where is everyone?" he whispered. "Where are all the other kids?"

The fire popped and crackled. Mr. Moon stepped into the orange light from the fireplace. He grinned at Tristan and his friends. His eyes moved slowly from one to the other.

The four of them stood awkwardly in the middle of the room.

"It's such a cold, windy night," Angela said, straightening a candle on the coffee table. "We thought it would be nice to have a fire."

"The house looks . . . awesome," Tristan said. He had his hands jammed into the pockets of his jeans. The mask over his eyes was really itching now.

"Yes, it's terrific," Rosa jumped in. "You must have worked so hard."

Angela smiled at her husband. "Yes, we want this to be our best Halloween party ever."

"Angela, let me introduce you to everyone," Mr. Moon said. "The wrestler is Ray. The mermaid is Rosa. This one is, um, Bella. And—"

He stopped as Michael entered the room.

Michael tugged his black cape behind him. His face was covered in white makeup. Thick black eyebrows had been painted over his tiny round eyes. He looked like a shorter, thinner version of his father.

So it *was* Michael outside a few minutes ago, Tristan realized.

"There you are!" Mr. Moon said. "Where were you? We were looking for you, Michael."

"Uh . . . nowhere really," Michael replied, gazing down at his shiny black shoes. "Just getting my costume ready."

"You know everybody—right?" Mr. Moon asked his son.

Michael nodded. "Do we have to have this party, Dad?" he asked, still not raising his eyes. "Can't we just stop it now?"

Rosa leaned close to Tristan. "He is really weird," she whispered.

Tristan shrugged.

"We're not stopping now. We've prepared so many surprises," Mr. Moon boomed. "You have to get into the party spirit, Michael."

Michael grumbled something Tristan couldn't hear.

Tristan's throat suddenly felt dry. He glanced around the living room but didn't see a refreshment table.

"Let's break the ice with a little game," Mr. Moon said, rubbing his hands together. His tiny eyes flashed inside his white, painted vampire face.

"Uh, shouldn't we wait for everyone else to show up?" Rosa asked.

Mr. Moon smiled. "Everyone is already here! You're the only people I invited!"

Tristan gasped.

"What kind of a freaky party is this?" Bella asked her friends quietly. Her voice shook slightly.

Angela disappeared into the next room, her halo bouncing on her head. A few seconds later, she returned carrying a large silver bowl.

Mr. Moon raised a black blindfold. "This should get us in a party mood. It is a guessing game," he announced. "I'm going to blindfold you one by one. Then I want you to feel what is in this bowl and tell me what you think it is."

"Yuck. It's going to be something really gross, isn't it?" Rosa said.

Mr. Moon chuckled. "That depends," he said. "One of you might not think it's so bad."

What does *that* mean? Tristan wondered.

Mr. Moon blindfolded Tristan first. Then he led him across the room to Angela.

Holding him by the wrist, the teacher lowered Tristan's hand into the bowl.

"Oh." Tristan's fingers wrapped around something cold and squishy. Wet. Kind of rubbery.

"Is it raw liver?" he asked.

"Keep feeling it. Move your hand around," Mr. Moon instructed.

Tristan felt around in the bowl. "It's kind of like cold, soft hot dogs," he said. "Yuck. Whatever it is, it's really slimy."

Mr. Moon led Tristan back across the room to the others. Then he blindfolded Bella.

She let out a gasp as her hand explored the bowl. "Yuck! Oh, gross. It's wet and cold. It *is* liver—isn't it!"

Angela laughed as she held the bowl. "Not quite. But you're warm," she said.

Rosa and Ray took their turns. When she felt the slimy, soft objects, Rosa's face turned nearly as green as her mermaid suit.

Ray didn't say a word. He dipped his hand around in the bowl. Then just shrugged.

Michael refused to take a turn. He sat glumly on the edge of the couch with his arms crossed tightly in front of him. "I already know what it is," he said.

"Everyone give up?" Mr. Moon asked. He took

the bowl from his wife. Then he tipped it so they all could see inside.

Tristan stared at the wet pile of yellow and red pieces. They looked like meat or maybe sausage wrappings.

"It's animal guts," Mr. Moon announced. "Real organs and intestines from animals that live in our woods."

"Ohhhh, sick," Bella groaned.

Ray laughed. "Cool."

Mr. Moon's eyes locked on Ray. "You think it's cool, huh? You don't think it's disgusting?"

"Well . . ." Ray hesitated.

"You *like* it?" Mr. Moon asked Ray eagerly.

"Uh . . . not exactly," Ray replied, confused.

Mr. Moon handed the bowl to Angela. Then he turned back to Tristan and his friends. "One of you *likes* animal guts—a lot," he said. "Because one of you is a *werewolf*!"

"Huh?"

"Excuse me?"

"What did he just say?"

The room erupted in cries of surprise.

Tristan's throat turned dry. He realized his hands were suddenly as cold as ice.

Mr. Moon had the strangest smile on his face. His tiny eyes sparkled excitedly in the firelight.

"This is going to be an exciting Halloween party,"

he said. "Because, as you know, it's not only Halloween—it's a full moon tonight."

Taking long, heavy strides, he stepped up close to the kids. His eyes moved from one to the other as his smile slowly faded.

Tristan jumped when he head the loud *click* of the doors locking.

He turned and saw heavy black metal bars slide downward and clang into place over the living room window.

He turned to Rosa with a frightened gasp.

Her chin was trembling. She chewed her bottom lip. Her eyes were narrowed on Mr. Moon.

"Someone in this room is a werewolf," the teacher said. "And we're not going to leave this house until we find out who it is."

"You—you're kidding, right?" Tristan blurted out.

"Yeah. It's a joke?" Ray asked. "You're just trying to scare us because it's Halloween?"

Mr. Moon's face went blank. "Why would I joke about such a serious thing?" he replied.

"We cannot allow a werewolf to run free," Angela said. "It's our duty to stop him. Or her."

Tristan pulled off his mask and folded it between his hands. "But this is crazy!" he cried. "We're kids. We're not werewolves. There's no such thing as werewolves!"

Mr. Moon studied him. "One of you is dangerous," he said softly. "One of you has made several attacks in this town. One of you is a werewolf! Is it *you*?"

"Me?" Tristan's voice cracked. "A werewolf? I don't think so."

The teacher turned to Ray. "You're the tough guy, right? Always looking for a fight?"

"Huh?" Ray gaped at him. "I'm just into the WWF, that's all."

Mr. Moon stared hard at Ray. "You just told us you enjoy feeling real animal body parts."

"That . . . that was a joke!" Ray stammered.

Mr. Moon turned to the girls.

Rosa and Bella took a step back. Bella's eyes were suddenly filled with fear.

"Who is it?" he demanded. "One of you? Why not step forward now and save us all a lot of time?"

"Is your dad joking?" Tristan turned to Michael.

But Michael had vanished from the room.

"We . . . we have to get home early," Rosa told the teacher.

"Yes. We all have a curfew," Tristan said. "We promised our parents."

Mr. Moon scratched the side of his face. The white vampire makeup on his cheek smeared onto his hand. He studied the smear on his fingers for a moment.

"I'm afraid you won't be home early," he told Rosa. He pointed to the window.

Through the bars, Tristan could see the moon still rising in the black night sky.

"The full moon won't reach its height till the clock strikes midnight," Mr. Moon said. "At that moment, the werewolf will be revealed to us all. I have no choice. I must keep you here until then."

"But we can't stay. We have an eleven o'clock curfew!" Tristan insisted.

The teacher shook his head. "You cannot leave."

"This is a joke. I know it is!" Bella cried. "But it isn't funny!"

She turned to Angela. "Can't you help us?"

Angela turned away.

"Let me show you something," Mr. Moon said. He motioned for the kids to follow him. He led them down a short hall.

Against the back wall stood a wire cage. The kind of cage pet stores use to hold very large dogs.

"This is where I will keep the werewolf," he announced. He slapped the top of the cage, making it ring. "The werewolf will stay here as my prisoner."

Tristan blinked. The man is serious, he realized. He is totally serious about this.

He plans to keep the four of us here until midnight. And *then* what?

Mr. Moon rubbed his hands together. The smile returned to his face. "Don't look so glum, everyone," he said. "This is a party. Let's have some fun."

Fun? Tristan thought.

He locks us in and bars the windows? Then he

tells us to have fun?

"Let's play some more games," Mr. Moon said, leading them back to the living room.

Tristan felt another chill of fear. "Games?" he asked. "What kind of games?"

The teacher narrowed his eyes at Tristan. "Werewolf games," he whispered.

"My wife and I will be right back," Mr. Moon said. "We have to prepare the next game. But—"

"We really have to leave now," Tristan interrupted. "We can't stay, Mr. Moon. Our parents will wonder what happened to us."

Mr. Moon pretended that Tristan hadn't spoken. "While Angela and I are out of the room getting ready, don't try to leave," he said.

"There is no way out," Angela added. Her smile never faded. It was frozen on her round pink face. "So don't waste your time trying to escape."

Her wings scraped the doorway as she followed her husband out of the room.

As soon as they were gone, Tristan turned to the

others. "Quick—there has to be a way out."

"He can't do this to us," Ray said angrily. He clenched his hands into fists. "They're both crazy."

"It has to be some kind of a sick joke," Bella said. "Totally sick."

"Do they really think one of us is going to turn into a werewolf at midnight?" Rosa asked. "Do they really think they're going to capture a werewolf and keep it locked up in that cage?"

"Of course not," Tristan said. "They're just trying to scare us." He swallowed. "And it's working. I'm pretty freaked out."

"Me, too," Bella confessed. "I mean, if they're really crazy, who knows *what* they will do?"

"And where did Michael go?" Ray asked.

"He tried to warn us," Tristan replied. "Remember? He kept telling us to be careful. He told us not to come here!"

"We're wasting time," Rosa said. "Quick—try the front door."

They ran to the front door.

Tristan reached it first and tried the knob. It wouldn't budge.

He turned the lock, then tried again.

"It's locked. This bolt won't move," he said. He used both hands to try to shove the heavy metal bolt. "No way."

Ray dove to the front window. He knocked over a

jack-o'-lantern. It bounced onto its side. The candle inside sizzled out.

Ray grabbed the metal bars over the window and tugged hard. "They're solid," he reported. "I can't move them."

Rosa made her way to another window and pushed back the curtains. "This one has bars, too," she said.

She wrapped her hands around the bars and pulled. She tried pulling them apart. Then she tried tugging the bars up.

They didn't budge.

"The back door!" Tristan cried. "Maybe they didn't lock the back door."

Rosa spun around. "Which way?" she cried. "This way?" She pointed to the back hall.

"There's another hall over here," Ray said. He took off, running through thick cobwebs, under the tangle of black and orange streamers.

Tristan and the two girls followed close behind. Tristan's heart was pounding. And his mouth was so dry, he couldn't swallow.

Please, he thought. Please, let us find a door that's open.

The hall was dark and narrow. Their shoes thudded on the hard floor. The hall ended at a closed wooden door.

"Where does this lead?" Bella asked.

"Only one way to find out," Ray said. He grabbed

the handle and pulled open the door.

"YAAAA-HAHAHAHAHA!"

A cackling monster—open, jagged-toothed jaw, bulging red eyes—burst out.

With a high shriek, it landed on Tristan and sent him sprawling to the floor.

"NO! PLEASE—NO!" Rosa screamed.

It—it's got me! Tristan struggled beneath the creature, kicking and thrashing.

Then he realized it was light. Too light to be a living thing.

He sat up and pushed the monster off easily.

Tristan scrambled to his feet and stared down at the ugly creature.

A costume.

A Halloween costume on a big stuffed animal. A big toy dog wearing a frightening rubber mask.

The cackling must have been on a tape or something, he realized.

He turned to his friends. They stared down at the monster costume. They were all breathing hard, their faces twisted in fear.

It fooled them, too, Tristan realized.

Mr. Moon has us all terrified.

"I'll bet he has the whole house rigged with surprises like that," Ray said.

"He wants to scare us to death," Bella added. "But why? Why is he doing this to us? He can't really think one of us is a werewolf—can he?"

"Bad news," Rosa said in a trembling voice. She poked her head into the next room. "There's no back door in here."

Tristan stepped up beside her and peered into the room. It was a small den. He saw a couch, two armchairs, a TV against the far wall.

Through the bars on the den window he could see the full moon. It had floated higher over the trees.

Midnight is drawing closer, he thought.

What's going to happen then?

"Where are you kids?" Mr. Moon was calling from the front of the house. "Come back to the living room. Don't waste your time trying to escape."

"He—he's coming after us," Bella whispered. Her eyes darted around, making a full circle, looking for a place to run.

Or hide.

"Don't make me angry, people!" Mr. Moon called. "This is supposed to be a party—remember?"

"Please don't make him angry," Angela shouted

from the front of the house. "Do as he says, kids. You don't know what he's like when he's angry!"

"What should we do?" Rosa whispered, glancing nervously down the hall.

Tristan spotted a black telephone on a table beside the couch.

"Maybe we can't escape," he said breathlessly. "But we can call for help."

He darted into the den and grabbed the phone.

He clicked it on. His hand trembled as he pressed the 911 emergency number.

Hurry! Hurry! he thought. *Someone answer!*

He heard Mr. Moon's heavy footsteps coming closer.

"Hello? May I help you?"

Yes! A woman's voice came on the line.

Tristan shouted desperately into the phone. "Please, help! This is an emergency! We're being held prisoner!"

"Prisoner?" the woman replied. "Can you give me an address?"

"Yes." He struggled to remember it. Suddenly his mind was a blank.

Finally it came back to him. Pressing the phone hard against his ear, Tristan told the operator the Moons' address.

"And you say you are being held prisoner in that house?" the woman asked.

"Yes. Four of us! He won't let us out of here." Tristan cried. "Hurry! Please! You've got to rescue us!"

"I'm sorry. I'd like to help you, but I can't," the woman said. "One of you is a werewolf."

Now Tristan recognized the woman's voice. Angela Moon.

Angrily, he tossed the phone to the floor.

"Are the police coming to rescue us?" Rosa asked.

Tristan shook his head. "No. It was another trick."

"Upstairs!" Ray cried. "Maybe there are windows we can open upstairs. We can lower ourselves out a window."

"Or maybe shout for help," Bella said.

Too late.

Mr. Moon burst into the hallway and came lumbering up to them.

Tristan saw that he was sweating hard. His white

vampire makeup had run onto the collar of his black jacket.

Mr. Moon spread the cape to block them from running past him. He glared at them angrily.

"You're not going anywhere," he said through gritted teeth. "You're staying until midnight. Don't you want to see which one of you turns into a werewolf?"

He didn't wait for an answer. He ushered everyone back to the living room.

As he followed his friends, Tristan thought hard.

Why does Mr. Moon suspect that one of us is a werewolf? he asked himself.

Did he hear Ray and me howling like wolves in the hall at school? Did that make him think we were werewolves?

Or did he see Bella eating fried chicken in the lunchroom—and chewing all the chicken bones? Does he think that makes Bella a werewolf?

Or is he just plain nuts?

Tristan didn't have long to think. Mr. Moon led them across the living room toward the fireplace. "Here is what we need for our next scary game," he said.

He pointed to a tall pile of dark fur objects in front of the fire.

At first Tristan thought he was staring at a stack of carpets. But as he moved closer, he realized it was a pile of animal skins.

"Do these look familiar to one of you?" Mr. Moon asked, eyeing them intently. "How about it? Has one of you seen skins like this before?"

No one replied.

Angela Moon looked on from the front doorway. She had removed her angel wings. But the gold halo still bobbed above her blond hair.

"These are werewolf skins," Mr. Moon announced.

Staring at the dark-furred skins, Rosa trembled and let out a soft cry.

"Gross," Bella muttered.

"These are the skins from werewolves Angela and I have captured in the past," Mr. Moon continued. His thick eyebrows moved up and down on his head like dark caterpillars. The firelight made his white vampire face glow orange and yellow.

"We keep the skins of all the werewolves we capture," Angela said from behind them. "Once we have their skin, they cannot go prowling any longer."

"We make sure the werewolf is powerless," Mr. Moon added. "Go ahead. Count the skins. Angela and I have been very successful."

Bella leaned close to Tristan. "They're not kidding," she whispered. "Those skins look like real wolf fur."

A shiver ran down Tristan's back. "We're going to play a game with these skins?" he asked.

Mr. Moon nodded. "A very simple game." A cold smile spread over his face.

"What do we have to do?" Rosa asked in a tiny voice.

"Put on the werewolf skins," Mr. Moon replied.

"No way," Ray muttered.

Bella had her hands pressed against the sides of her face. She stared at the pile of dark fur. "But . . . but they're disgusting," she whispered.

Tristan jumped as Mr. Moon screamed at the top of his lungs: *You heard me! Put on the skins— NOW!*

"Don't lose your temper, dear," Angela said from across the room. "You know it isn't good for you."

"I'm not kidding around here," Mr. Moon snapped angrily. "I'm going to trap a werewolf tonight. If you kids don't cooperate, you could *all* end up in the cage with it."

Angela crossed the room and stepped up beside the animal skins. She put a hand on her husband's shoulder. "Don't put them in the cage yet. Give them another chance. It's supposed to be a party—right?"

Angela motioned for Tristan to take a werewolf skin.

He grabbed the one off the top with both hands. His fingers sank into the bristly fur.

The skin was a lot heavier than he imagined. The fur felt scratchy and tough, like thousands of little nails. Patches of gray skin showed through.

"Ohh." Tristan groaned as a sharp odor greeted his nose. "It stinks!"

The skin smelled like rotting food.

Rosa held a ratty-looking skin up in front of her. "This is *so* sick," she moaned.

"Put them on," Mr. Moon ordered. "Hurry."

Ray slid his skin over his shoulders. "Are you sure this is a wolf skin? It smells like a skunk," he complained, holding his nose.

Bella had her eyes shut. She held her skin as far away from her as she could. "I'm going to be sick. Really. I'm . . . I'm going to lose my dinner."

Her teeth clenched tightly, Rosa pulled her skin around her. "Oh, no. It's crawling with bugs." She began to twist and squirm.

Tristan still clutched his skin in front of him. He took a deep breath and held it. Then he pulled the heavy fur around his shoulders.

The fur bristled the back of his neck. Tristan felt his back start to itch.

He couldn't hold his breath any longer. He let it out in a long *whoosh*.

The odor of the skin rose around him. He gagged. Struggled to keep his stomach from lurching.

The skin weighed heavily on his back. Gripping

the ends with his hands, he felt bugs crawl over him.

"How long do we have to wear these things?" he asked Mr. Moon.

"This is so sick," Bella moaned. She slapped at her side. "The bugs are *biting!*"

"Pull the skins tighter," the teacher ordered.

"Yes. Let us see what you look like," Angela said, still smiling that frozen smile.

With a sigh, Tristan pulled the wolf skin tighter around him.

Beside him, Rosa was breathing hard, her whole body shaking. "I'll never get this rotten smell off me," she whispered.

Bella slapped at a bug. She had tears running down her cheeks. Mr. Moon stepped up and adjusted the skin over her back. "Tighter," he said. "Come on, Bella. Pull it tighter."

"It really itches," Ray groaned. "Can we stop now?"

Mr. Moon studied each of them one at a time.

"What's the point of this?" Tristan cried. "Why are we wearing these ratty skins?"

"I want to see who looks the most comfortable in a wolf skin," the teacher replied. He brought his face close to Tristan. "You look pretty comfortable in yours. Maybe you've worn a wolf skin before? On nights of the full moon?"

"You're crazy," Tristan replied sharply.

Mr. Moon's eyes bulged. His face reddened. "Don't

ever say that to me again!" he bellowed. "I know what I'm doing here."

He pointed to the stack of skins. "Do you see all the werewolves I have captured?"

"Easy, dear," Angela said. She raised a small silvery camera to her eye. "Stand still, everyone. I have to take your picture."

She aimed at Ray first.

The white flash made Tristan blink. His arms and back itched from the heavy fur. He felt bugs crawling up into his hair.

"This boy over here looks pretty comfortable," Angela said.

Tristan raised his eyes in time to be caught by another flash of light. It took him a while to realize that Angela was talking about *him*.

Still blinking, he saw Mr. Moon and his wife both studying him. Mr. Moon stepped forward and adjusted the skin over Tristan, pulling it higher on his shoulders.

"Mmmmmm, yes," he said, rubbing his white chin. The makeup came off on his hand. "Yes, you look very comfortable in fur, Tristan."

The teacher grabbed Tristan by the shoulders. His hands pressed down roughly on the bristly skin. He lowered his face and stared Tristan in the eye.

"Is there anything you would like to tell us?" he demanded. "Is there something you'd like to share with the rest of the group?"

Tristan tried to move away. But the teacher gripped him tightly.

The putrid smell of the animal skin swirled around Tristan. He suddenly felt sick, dizzy.

The heavy skin seemed to press down on him. His legs began to shake. Then his knees folded and he dropped to the carpet.

"Let's hear you howl," Mr. Moon said.

The teacher was breathing hard now, his face wide with excitement. Sweat poured down the white vampire makeup. His black eyebrows waggled up and down, as if he had lost control of them.

"Come on, Tristan. Let's hear a real wolf howl," he urged, clapping his hands.

Angela snapped another photo of Tristan. "Go ahead. You can do it. Just open your mouth and howl like a wolf."

"You know you want to," Mr. Moon said, eyes flashing excitedly beneath the dark, wriggling eyebrows. "You know you want to let out a real wolf howl. The way you do *every* full moon!"

"Tristan isn't a werewolf," Bella cried angrily. "Stop accusing him!"

"Leave Tristan alone!" Ray said. He pulled off the wolf skin and dropped it back on the pile of skins.

Mr. Moon spun around to face Ray. "Yes, maybe you're right," he said. "Maybe Tristan isn't a werewolf. Maybe *you* are!"

Angela flashed another photo of Ray. "Let's hear you give it a try, Ray," she said.

"Howl for us, Ray," Mr. Moon ordered. "Go ahead. Let's hear it. Just the way you howled in school the other day."

"Huh?" Ray's mouth dropped open.

"Did you think I didn't hear you?" Mr. Moon asked. "I've heard you howl in school. You can't keep it inside, can you! You can't hide your animal feelings."

"You—you're crazy!" Ray declared. He crossed his tattooed arms in front of him. "We want to go home now," he told Mr. Moon, staring hard at him. "We're not going to play your games anymore."

Mr. Moon leaned close to Ray. "We don't want the werewolf to escape—do we? If I don't capture it, it may harm innocent people tonight."

"But we're not werewolves!" Ray screamed.

"Prove it," Mr. Moon replied. "Go ahead. Prove it. Let's hear you howl."

Ray let out a disgusted sigh. Then he opened his mouth and howled at the top of his lungs.

Mr. Moon nodded thoughtfully. "Very good." He turned to Rosa. "Now you."

Rosa shook her head. "This is crazy."

"You're going to be in major trouble when we get out of this house," Tristan said to the teacher.

"I don't think so," Mr. Moon replied. "The police will thank me when I capture a werewolf." He pointed to the pile of skins on the floor. "The police always thank me."

"Come on, everyone," Angela chimed in. "Let's get into it. Let's get in a party spirit."

"They're both *sick*," Rosa muttered to Tristan.

"Everybody, howl," Mr. Moon ordered. "At the count of three. Everyone!"

They had no choice. They tossed back their heads and howled like wolves.

The high wails rang out through the house. The windows rattled against the metal bars. Tristan covered his ears over the shrill sounds.

Maybe some neighbors will hear, he thought.

Maybe neighbors will hear our cries and wonder what is going on. Maybe they'll call the police or come over to check it out.

"Very good! Very good!" Angela snapped a few more photos.

She turned to her husband. "What do you think?"

He rubbed his chin. "I think I know who the werewolf is," he said.

"I still have my eye on Tristan," Mr. Moon said. He narrowed his eyes at Tristan, studying him hard.

Tristan shuddered.

This can't be happening, he thought.

He glanced out the window. The moon hung high in the black sky, bright and full.

It's getting late, Tristan realized.

Mr. Moon rubbed his chin thoughtfully. "But Bella could also be the one," he said.

Bella uttered a startled cry. "Huh? Me?"

"She howled as if she had done it before," Mr. Moon told his wife.

"I agree," Angela said.

Mr. Moon nodded, his eyes on Bella. "As I listened,

I could picture her covered in wolf fur. Running on all fours. Howling at the moon. And then—pouncing. Pouncing on an innocent victim. Attacking . . . attacking."

"*No way!*" Bella screamed.

Rosa put an arm around her trembling shoulders. "It's okay," she whispered. "Don't let him frighten you."

Bella let out a sob. "This is a bad joke," she cried. "It's all a bad joke."

"It *isn't* a joke!" Mr. Moon screamed. "It's serious. You wouldn't call it a joke if you were a werewolf's victim! You wouldn't call it a joke if you were torn to pieces by a raging wolf creature!"

"Take it easy, dear," Angela said. "Take a deep breath. You know how you get."

Mr. Moon glanced at the clock on the mantel. "Ten-fifteen," he said. "Our werewolf will soon start to change. Once it is captured, the rest of you can all go home."

"Let us go home now!" Ray cried. "This is a total waste of time."

"You won't get away with it," Bella said in a trembling voice.

Once again Mr. Moon pointed to the pile of skins on the floor. "That's what *they* said!" He started toward the door. "I think it's time for the next test."

He returned a few seconds later carrying a large

wooden crate. The crate had FRAGILE stenciled all over it in big black letters. A yellow label on the side read: ISLAND OF BORNEO.

Mr. Moon dropped the carton to the floor with a heavy *thud*. He pulled a claw hammer from his back pocket and began to pry open the lid.

"I think you will find these little guys interesting," he said, struggling with the lid. "They come all the way from the South Seas."

Tristan heard soft squeaking sounds from inside the carton. What does he have in there? he wondered. Some kind of animal?

Mr. Moon gave a hard tug with the hammer. Wood cracked as the lid pulled back.

"Hey—no!" he screamed as four little brown creatures jumped out.

They were round. About the size of a softball. Their long, pointed quills brushed the carpet as they ran.

"Are they porcupines?" Tristan asked.

The Moons chased after them. Angela dove to the floor and made a wild grab.

But the creature darted out of her grasp and disappeared into the hall.

She stood up, holding a handful of brown quills. "They're all getting away!" she screamed.

Mr. Moon spun in a circle, ready to capture them. But the four round creatures had scooted out of the room in different directions.

Tristan could hear their squeaks as they vanished down the back hallways.

Mr. Moon lumbered to the carton, leaned over it, and peered inside. "Ah-ha! One little guy didn't get away," he said.

The teacher reached into the carton. He lifted out the small round animal and held it tightly between his hands. "You wanted to stay and play, didn't you!" Mr. Moon declared.

Tristan stared hard at the creature. It reminded him of a Koosh Ball, round and covered with long, prickly fur. Its face was completely hidden behind its quills.

Holding it carefully in front of him, Mr. Moon carried it over to Tristan and his friends. "Cute little guy, huh?" The teacher smiled, his eyes flashing with excitement.

"It's called a plog," he explained. "It comes from the island of Borneo, many thousands of miles from here."

Bella eyed it suspiciously. "What are we going to do with it?" she asked in a tiny, frightened voice.

Mr. Moon's smile grew wider. "Plogs are very gentle, very sweet-natured," he replied. He stroked the creature's quills with one finger. "See how much he likes to be petted?"

He lifted the plog close to Bella's face. She jumped back with a short cry.

"The plogs have only one natural enemy," Mr. Moon continued. "The werewolf. They are quiet and tame most of the time. But if a werewolf is near, they attack. And so the people of Borneo use these little guys as werewolf hunters."

"Enough talk," Angela said, crossing the room. "Let's pass the plog around. Let's see who our werewolf is."

"Pass it around?" Tristan asked, taking a step back.

"It will attack only if you are a werewolf," Mr. Moon replied, staring hard at Tristan. "So you have nothing to fear—right?"

"None of us has anything to fear!" Tristan cried. "We're not werewolves."

He lowered his gaze to the round, quilled animal between the teacher's hands. "You really think we'll believe that this little thing is a werewolf hunter? It's just a porcupine or a hedgehog or something."

"Then you won't be afraid to take him," Mr. Moon said, his smile fading. He shoved the plog into Tristan's hand. "Go ahead. Hold him."

Tristan had no choice. He took the plog into his hands. It felt warm and prickly. The quills were hard. The points scratched his hands.

He could feel the plog's rapid heartbeat. Through the thick carpet of quills he could see tiny, round black eyes staring out at him.

"The plog isn't interested in you," Mr. Moon said, frowning as if disappointed. "Pass it to Ray."

Tristan hesitated. "Do you want it?"

Ray held out his hands. "Sure. No problem. Hand it over."

Ray held the plog for a full minute. "It's kind of tickly," he said. "It makes my hands itch."

"Pass it to Bella," Mr. Moon instructed.

Bella let out a sharp gasp. "No way," she said, shaking her head.

"Pass it to Bella," the teacher repeated softly.

Ray held the plog up to her. Bella stepped back and raised both hands in the air.

"No. I won't take it! I won't! You can't make me. I won't take it!"

Mr. Moon took the plog from Ray. Holding it in front of him, he stepped up close to Bella. "And why won't you take it?" he asked softly.

Bella had her arms crossed in front of her. "Because it's dumb," she answered. "This whole thing is dumb. I want to go home."

"But now we all think you are the werewolf," Mr. Moon said. "Now we all think it is you, Bella. Don't we?"

"No way," Ray replied.

"We all agree with Bella," Rosa said. "This is dumb."

Mr. Moon turned and stared at Rosa as if seeing her for the first time. "Almost forgot about you," he said. "Here. You take it."

He pushed the plog into Rosa's hands before she could back away. She cupped the creature in her hands and held it up in front of her face.

"Are you satisfied now?" she asked Mr. Moon angrily. "I'm holding it—okay? See? It's not doing anything. It—*ouch*!"

Rosa let out a cry of pain as the creature sank its teeth into the palm of her hand.

"It *bit* me!" she screeched.

The plog dropped from her hands.

Mr. Moon dove for it. But it shot out of the room and vanished into the hall leading to the kitchen.

"Now they've *all* run away," Angela said, shaking her head.

"We'll round them up later," Mr. Moon said. Rosa was smoothing a finger over her injured palm. Mr. Moon grabbed her by the arm. "It seems we may have caught our werewolf," he said.

"You're *both* insane! Totally insane!" Rosa screamed.

"If we're insane, why did the plog bite only you?" the teacher demanded.

"I don't know. Let *go* of me!" Rosa jerked her arm free.

"Calm down, everyone," Angela said. "Do you need a bandage for that hand, Rosa?"

"She doesn't need a bandage," Mr. Moon said.

"In a short while she'll be growing wolf fur over the cut."

"I think it's snack time," Angela said, her eyes on Rosa's hand. "Anybody hungry?"

No one answered.

"Oh, come on," she said. "Everybody likes special treats on Halloween."

"Come into the dining room," Mr. Moon said. "We've prepared some very tasty treats for you."

Tristan and Rosa hung back as the others trooped to the dining room.

"Is your hand okay?" Tristan whispered.

Rosa nodded. "Just two little puncture holes. That stupid plog has sharp teeth."

"There has to be a way out of this house," Tristan said.

"I don't want to stay here another minute," Rosa replied.

"We've got to try upstairs," Tristan whispered. "Or maybe the basement."

"But—how?" Rosa whispered back.

"Hurry, you two," Mr. Moon called to them. "Stay with the group. Don't try anything funny, Tristan. Don't try to help the werewolf escape."

The long table had been set with an orange-and-black tablecloth. A silver platter was placed in the center of the table.

What is that piled on the platter? Tristan wondered.

He squinted at it, trying to make out what it held.

"Oh, gross," he groaned when he realized what it was.

He stared at the stack of red and purple raw meat.

"A nice assortment of animal guts," Angela said, grinning her sick grin. "I'm sure you remember them from our little guessing game before?"

"We don't want good meat to go to waste," Mr. Moon added. "Come on, kids. Fill up your plates."

He grabbed a disgusting, shiny pink intestine off the platter and shoved it into Rosa's face. "Go ahead. You know you love it. Start eating."

"You—you really want us to eat that stuff?" Tristan gasped.

Angela handed him a china dinner plate piled high with raw meat.

Rosa turned away from Mr. Moon. "Raw animal organs? No. Please . . ." She held her stomach.

Angela plopped a slimy purple blob of meat on Tristan's plate. "Go ahead. Eat up."

"No way!" Tristan cried.

Beside him, Ray stared at the yellow intestine section on his plate. With an angry growl he picked it up and heaved it across the dining room.

It made a wet *splat* on the wallpaper and bounced to the wooden floor.

Mr. Moon stepped in front of Ray. "Didn't your parents teach you not to play with your food?" he asked.

The teacher lifted a shiny purple organ off the tray—and shoved it into Ray's mouth. "Eat. Go ahead. You know you want it. You know you love it."

Ray made a loud gulping sound as the raw wet meat slid down his throat. Then he bent to the floor and started to retch.

Mr. Moon turned to Tristan. "Do I have to feed you, too?" he barked.

Tristan saw that he had no choice.

He picked up the wet raw meat in one hand. It's so cold, he thought. Maybe I can choke it down without tasting it.

He raised it to his mouth. He took a deep breath and held it.

He pushed it into his mouth.

Ohhhh. It's too big to swallow whole, he realized.

He bit into it. It was soft and squishy, like raw liver.

He tried to chew it.

But his stomach heaved. He gagged. Then he bent over and spewed it out.

"You're pretending," Mr. Moon said, standing over him. "You love the taste of raw animal guts, don't you, Tristan?"

Tristan tasted the sour meat on his tongue. He gagged again.

"Why don't you admit it, Tristan?" Mr. Moon continued excitedly. "Why don't you admit that you are the werewolf and allow your friends to go home?"

Still bent over, Tristan struggled to catch his breath. Why is he picking on me? he wondered.

What can I do?

How can I prove to him that I'm not the werewolf?

When he straightened up, Tristan saw Bella choking down a long yellow intestine. She had her eyes shut. She was chewing rapidly, swallowing, swallowing, swallowing.

"She likes it!" Mr. Moon screamed happily. He clapped his hands. "See? She likes it!"

"Maybe Bella is our werewolf," Angela said.

Bella finished the intestine and hunched over, gasped for breath.

Once again Tristan pictured her in the lunchroom at school, chewing the fried chicken bones.

That doesn't make Bella a werewolf, he thought.

I know Bella isn't a werewolf.

Bella *can't* be a werewolf.

Bella was holding her stomach, still swallowing rapidly. Trying to get the awful taste from her mouth.

"Ohhhhh!"

With a sharp cry, she turned and vomited the yellow stuff onto the rug.

"Perhaps everyone needs a drink," Mr. Moon suggested. "As soon as Rosa has her snack, we will bring you all something delightful."

What will it be? Tristan wondered. Blood?

Rosa had a red, heart-shaped blob on her plate. She tried to raise it to her mouth.

But it slid out of her hand. It hit the floor and bounced under the table.

"Gross," Rosa muttered, her face twisted in disgust. "It's so slimy and cold."

Angela handed her another red piece of raw meat. "Don't waste food, dear," she scolded. "Come on. Down the hatch. We're all waiting."

"I—I can't!" Rosa cried.

"*Eat it—NOW!*" Mr. Moon bellowed.

Closing her eyes, Rosa tried to nibble a tiny piece of it. But her stomach lurched, and she tossed it to the floor beside the other one.

"They don't like my cooking!" Angela joked.

Mr. Moon had his eyes on Tristan. "One of them likes it," he said. "One of them is pretending it makes him sick."

He stared a long while at Tristan. Then he turned

and studied Rosa again.

"I'll get the drinks," Angela said. She picked up the platter, still piled high with raw animal parts. Then she disappeared into the kitchen.

"It's getting late," Mr. Moon said. "I know the werewolf wants to go out trick-or-treating. To find an innocent victim for his goodie bag."

He slammed his fist on the dining room table. "But not tonight!" he bellowed. "The werewolf will spend Halloween in a cage!"

Tristan took a deep breath, trying to slow his racing heartbeat. The toy guns at his waist suddenly felt heavy. He had completely forgotten he was in costume.

He pulled off the holsters and tossed them against the wall. Then he tore the red bandanna off his neck.

The others had taken apart their costumes, too.

Angela returned carrying another tray. This one contained four silver goblets.

"After that special treat, I'm sure you are all thirsty," Mr. Moon said.

Angela set the tray down on the table. Then she handed a goblet to each kid.

Tristan peered at the dark, wine-colored liquid in the silver cup. He raised it to his nose and sniffed it.

A slightly sweet aroma.

"Don't worry. It doesn't taste bad," Mr. Moon

said. "In fact, I think you will like the taste."

"What is it?" Ray asked, staring into his cup. "It isn't blood—is it?"

Mr. Moon laughed. "Would you like that, Ray? Would you like a nice, warm cup of fresh blood right now? Is that what you crave?"

Ray rolled his eyes. "I just asked," he replied. "I mean . . . it *looks* like blood."

"The moon is getting high, Ray," Mr. Moon said, motioning to the barred window. "Are you starting to feel yourself change? Are you starting to feel your wolf nature rise? Are you suddenly hungry for a nice drink of blood?"

Ray shook his head and didn't answer.

Holding her silver goblet in front of her, Bella stepped up to Mr. Moon. "What are you going to do when the clock strikes midnight and no one turns into a werewolf?" she asked. "What are you going to do then?"

Mr. Moon gazed at the pile of skins on the floor in the next room. He turned a cold smile on Bella. "I've never been wrong before," he said softly.

"Drink up, everyone," Angela said cheerfully.

"What you hold in your goblets is called *wolf-bane*," Mr. Moon explained. "One of you has probably been warned about wolfbane. It's an herb discovered by people in the forests of middle Europe."

"It's used to keep werewolves away," Angela added.

"It's one of the few things that works against them."

"Yes. Werewolves are allergic to wolfbane," Mr. Moon said. "It poisons them. They cannot drink it."

Tristan gazed into the goblet. He tilted it slightly. The dark liquid was thick, like motor oil.

"Angela and I mixed the wolfbane herb in the liquid ourselves. It's a very strong mixture—instant death for a werewolf," Mr. Moon said.

He motioned for them to raise their glasses. "We're all going to drink now," he said.

Once again his eyes moved down the line of kids and came to rest on Tristan.

"Three of you will drink the wolfbane down easily. One of you won't be able to drink it. And then we will know. We will know. . . ."

Tristan glanced at Ray. Ray made a disgusted face as he raised the goblet.

Rosa had her eyes on Tristan. She tilted the cup toward him as if making a toast.

"Drink up," Mr. Moon ordered. "Now. Drink up, everyone. The cage is waiting. Let's see who our werewolf is tonight."

Tristan lifted the rim of the cup to his lips—

—and the doorbell rang.

Mr. Moon and his wife turned to the front hall. "Who could that be?" Angela asked.

"Don't anyone move," Mr. Moon ordered.

They both hurried to the door.

Tristan set his cup on the table. "Come on—" he whispered. "This is our chance. Let's get *out* of here!"

"Now we can try the kitchen," Ray said.

No one said another word. They all set their goblets on the table and took off.

Tristan found his way into the kitchen. He ran past the disgusting tray of animal parts on the counter.

The kitchen had one narrow window looking onto the backyard. Tristan tugged back the curtains.

"Oh, no."

The window was barred like all the others.

Ray hurried to the kitchen door and struggled to open it. He twisted the brass knob one way, then the other. He tried pulling. Then he lowered his shoulder to the door and pushed hard.

"It won't budge," he groaned.

"The doors are bolted electronically," Tristan said. "Like the bars on the windows."

"There has to be a way out!" Bella cried. "I—I can't stand this anymore!"

Rosa placed a hand on Bella's shoulder. "Don't worry. We'll get out," she said.

"But—how?" Ray cried, glancing around the big room frantically.

"The basement!" Tristan cried. "Maybe there is a way out through the basement."

"If there are windows . . ." Ray muttered.

"But how do we get there?" Rosa asked, spinning around to search.

Tristan spotted a narrow hallway leading off the kitchen. "One of these doors has got to lead downstairs."

They took off again.

As they ran, Tristan could hear Mr. Moon and Angela at the front door.

"What great costumes!"

"Very scary!"

"What are you supposed to be? A mummy?"

They were oohing and ahing over trick-or-treaters passing out candy.

We should have screamed for help, Tristan realized. Maybe the trick-or-treaters would have helped us.

Maybe they have a parent along with them. We should have run to the front door and shouted.

Too late.

He heard the front door slam.

Rosa pulled open a door at the end of the short hall. "Yes! Here it is!" she cried. "Basement stairs."

They didn't hesitate. They made their way down the stairs. Tristan shut the hall door behind him as he followed the others down.

The basement air felt cold and damp. Tristan heard the steady *drip drip drip* of water somewhere in the distance.

A huge gray furnace as big as a small house rumbled in the center of the room. It was surrounded by mountains of junk.

Piles of old newspapers and magazines. Stacks of old clothing. Beat-up furniture. Cardboard cartons piled to the ceiling.

"Check it out. That window isn't barred," Rosa said, pointing.

Tristan gazed at the small window. It was at the basement ceiling, at ground level.

Was it big enough to climb through?

He heard the ceiling creak overhead. He knew that Mr. Moon and Angela were searching for them upstairs.

We have only a few seconds, he realized.

Ray stood under the tiny window, gazing up at it. "It's pretty small," he said.

"The rest of us are too big. But you can squeeze through," Rosa told him.

"I'll give you a boost," Tristan said.

He cupped his hands and allowed Ray to place one shoe in them. Then he tried to hoist him up the stone wall toward the window.

"Whoa." Tristan cried out as Ray slid back to the floor. "You're too heavy," he groaned.

"I couldn't reach anyway," Ray said. He ran across the room. He grabbed a milk crate and slid it under the window.

Tristan slid another one over to it and piled it on top of the first. "Okay. Climb up." He gave Ray another boost, onto the top of the crates.

Ray started to reach for the window handle—when they all heard a cough.

Behind them, something crashed to the floor. A carton?

"What was that?" Rosa asked.

Tristan turned to the stairs. Mr. Moon?

No.

He heard another cough. Then footsteps coming toward them.

"Someone is here with us!" Tristan cried. "We're not alone down here!"

They all gasped as Michael Moon stepped into the light.

He had tried to wipe off the vampire makeup. But patches of white clung to his cheeks and chin. His hair was still slicked back on his head. He had changed into jeans and a gray sweatshirt.

"I—I thought you were my parents," he said, glancing to the stairs.

"They'll be here any second," Tristan told him. "You have to help us."

"I tried to warn you," Michael said. "You should have listened."

"We didn't know," Rosa told him. "We had no idea that your parents—"

"They've done this before," Michael interrupted.

"You mean—capture a real werewolf?" Tristan asked.

"They do it every year," Michael answered. "I tried to stop them this time. I really did. But they wouldn't listen."

"How can we get out?" Ray asked. "Can you help me up to that window?"

"The window up there doesn't open," Michael replied, frowning up at it. "You'd have to break the glass. And there isn't time."

He gazed down at Rosa's hand. "Those puncture marks. Don't tell me—" His face filled with horror.

"A plog bit me," Rosa said. "Your father had them in a big carton. He said—"

"Did he put them back in their box?" Michael asked. "He didn't let them escape this time—did he?"

"They all escaped," Tristan told Michael. "What difference does it make? We have to hurry. We—"

"Oh, wow." Michael Moon shook his head. "This is bad. *Really* bad. They turn into hunters," he said, staring at Rosa's hand. "After they've been free for a short while. They need meat. They're tiny—but they become so vicious, so deadly."

Tristan jumped when he heard a soft *thud* behind him.

He turned—and saw them. Five plogs, moving silently across the basement.

Coming from all directions.

Their dark quills stood straight up. Their tiny eyes glared coldly from between the quills.

Michael ducked behind a stack of cartons as the plogs attacked.

All five of them jumped at once. With high squeals, they leaped into the air.

"Hey!" Tristan screamed as one of them hit the front of his shirt—and stuck.

He felt a stab of pain as the sharp points poked through his shirt into his skin.

"No!" he grabbed it with both hands and heaved it across the basement.

"Help me! Help!" Bella shrieked.

She was struggling to pull a plog from her hair. "Owww! It's digging into my head!"

Two plogs had attached to Ray's tights. He kicked his leg back and forth and slapped at them, trying to knock them off.

Tristan spotted another stairway half-hidden in shadow at the back of the basement. "This way!" he cried.

He ducked as a plog leaped for his head. It flew over him and hit the stone basement wall with a soft *splat*.

Tristan took off, running to the other stairway. Glancing back, he saw Rosa help rip a plog from Bella's hair.

Then all four of them were running to the stairs. Taking the stairs two at a time.

Tristan turned and saw the five plogs following after them, sliding over the basement floor, quills raised.

Gasping for breath, Tristan pushed open the door at the top and kept running.

The long, dark hall had rooms on both sides. Tristan passed a small home office . . . a bathroom . . . bedrooms.

"Where does this lead?" Rosa asked breathlessly.

The hall ended suddenly at a tall, dark door. The four of them stopped outside it, breathing noisily.

They turned and saw the plogs, moving in a group now. Scooting toward them down the hall.

"Quick—open it," Bella urged. "Hurry!"

Tristan grabbed the doorknob.

But a sound on the other side made him jump back.

He heard a hard *bump* against the door.

He heard something pawing the floor.

Scraping sounds.

Animal panting.

Another hard bump on the door.

And then a low growl.

"Oh."

Bella's mouth dropped open in fear. "No, wait! Don't open it, Tristan."

They listened to the frantic pawing sounds on the other side of the door. The low growls.

"A werewolf," Ray muttered. "They've already captured one. There's a werewolf in there."

"Don't open it," Bella repeated.

Another growl.

Tristan turned. The plogs had pressed together to form a line. They were preparing to leap.

We're trapped, Tristan realized.

I have no choice.

He grabbed the door, held his breath, and pulled it open.

A dog! Tristan realized.

An enormous black Lab.

Panting hard, the dog burst into the hallway.

It ran past Tristan and his friends, big paws thudding on the hard floor.

With a growl, it attacked the plogs.

It lifted one of the prickly round creatures in its teeth and tossed it against the wall. The plog squealed as it hit the wall, then leaped away.

Squeaking loudly, the other four plogs scattered, darting down the hall after the first one.

Barking at the top of its lungs, the big dog bounded after them. It turned a corner and disappeared.

"I see you let Bully out," a voice boomed. Mr.

Moon stepped into the hall. "You really shouldn't have done that."

"Let us go!" Ray screamed. "Those animals—they dug their teeth into us and bit us!"

Bella had her hands on the sides of her head. "My hair. Did they tear out my hair?"

"It's okay," Rosa told her.

"I'm going to call Bully back," Mr. Moon said. "Bully is a good dog. But he doesn't like werewolves. In fact, Bully becomes truly vicious when there is a werewolf in the room."

The teacher's eyes flashed. "Shall I call Bully back?"

"No—please! Tristan cried, tossing up his hands. "Enough. That's enough. You can let my friends go. I confess! It's me! I'm a werewolf!"

Tristan's friends all gasped.

"Wait! Don't call the dog back—please," Tristan begged. "You've caught me. I'm the one."

"Tristan—what are you *saying*?" Bella cried.

"It's true," Tristan said, raising his right hand as if swearing an oath. "He has caught me. I don't know how you knew. But I'm a werewolf."

Mr. Moon nodded. His grin grew wider. "Another victory," he muttered. He moved quickly to capture Tristan.

Tristan backed against the wall. "You're going to put me in the cage—right?" he asked.

The teacher nodded. "It's almost midnight. I need to lock you up before you start to change."

"And this means you can let everyone else go home?" Tristan asked. "You've got me. I have confessed. So you can let my friends go right now?"

Rosa stared hard at Tristan. He could see her thinking hard.

Does she realize what I'm trying to do? he wondered.

If Mr. Moon allows the others to leave, they can go bring back help. They can bring someone to rescue me.

Rosa stepped in front of Tristan. "I—I want to confess, too," she told Mr. Moon.

"Really?" He couldn't hide his surprise.

"I'm a werewolf, too," Rosa said. "That's why Tristan and I are such good friends. Because we're both werewolves."

"Really?" Mr. Moon repeated. His eyes moved excitedly from Rosa to Tristan. He rubbed his hands together. "Well, well. This is a lucky night. *Two* werewolves for the price of one!"

He clapped his hands on their shoulders and began guiding them down the hall.

"Are you taking us to the cages?" Tristan asked. "Does this mean that Bella and Ray can go home?"

Mr. Moon didn't reply. He brought them all to the kitchen.

Angela was seated on a high stool at the kitchen counter. She held a white mug of coffee between her hands.

She had finally removed her halo. Her blond hair was still piled high on her head. And she hadn't changed from her white angel robe.

Angela took a sip of coffee and set down the mug. "What's happening?" she asked her husband.

"We have captured *two* werewolves tonight!" Mr. Moon declared. He shoved Tristan and Rosa forward. "These two have confessed."

"How wonderful!" Angela exclaimed.

She glanced at the kitchen clock. It read eleven-thirty. "This means we will have them in the cage before they can do any harm tonight."

"And it means Bella and Ray can go home—right?" Tristan repeated.

Please let them go, he thought.

Please let them go get someone to rescue Rosa and me from these two lunatics.

"We can't let them go just yet," Mr. Moon said. "Not until I know for sure that you and Rosa are telling the truth."

"But we've confessed!" Rosa cried. "We are the werewolves. Why would we lie about it?"

"Lock us up before midnight," Tristan warned. "Hurry. Rosa and I don't want to hurt any innocent people tonight."

"And let our friends go home," Rosa said.

Mr. Moon didn't reply. He led all four of them back into the dining room.

"I will let them go," he said, "as soon as you prove you are werewolves."

Tristan gasped. "Huh? Prove it?"

Mr. Moon picked up a silver goblet from the dining room table. He handed it to Tristan.

"I believe we were all about to have a little drink of wolfbane," he said. "But we got interrupted."

Tristan stared at the dark red liquid in the cup. His heart started to pound.

"Pick up your glasses, everyone," Mr. Moon instructed. "Let's drink it down."

"Do Ray and I have to drink it, too?" Bella asked.

Mr. Moon nodded. "Everyone drinks the wolfbane," he said. "If Tristan and Rosa are telling the truth, they will instantly become very sick. If they are lying—or if someone else is the secret werewolf—we will know it at once."

"Wolfbane makes werewolves very, very sick," Angela said, standing in the doorway.

"Go ahead. Prove it," Mr. Moon said to Tristan and Rosa. "Prove that you are telling the truth. Let's see if the wolfbane poisons you."

Tristan and Rosa gazed across the table at each other. Tristan could see Rosa's hand tremble. She gripped the goblet in both hands.

Tristan dipped a finger into the liquid. It felt warm and thick, thicker than maple syrup.

He glanced at the grandfather clock in the corner.

Only twenty minutes until midnight arrived.

"Come on, everybody. It's getting late," Mr. Moon said. "I know some of you want to get home. And some of you need to be locked away in the cage."

"Drink up, everyone!" Angela said.

Tristan took a deep breath.

Then he raised the glass to his lips and started to drink.

The liquid felt warm and thick in Tristan's mouth. He tried to swallow it quickly. But it had big lumps in it that stuck to his tongue and the roof of his mouth.

He turned and gazed at his friends. Bella had the silver cup to her lips. She was taking short sips, her face twisted in disgust.

Ray tilted his goblet and tried to swallow the wolfbane in one gulp. But he started to choke and spit out a thick red glob.

"It tastes like garbage!" Ray cried. The red liquid oozed down his chin.

"Drink up," Mr. Moon said sharply. "If you waste it, I'll just pour another cup for you. Come on, down the hatch. Drink up, everyone!"

"There is plenty for everyone!" Angela exclaimed.

"All four of you must drink at least one cup," Mr. Moon ordered.

Rosa had the goblet pressed to her mouth. She swallowed noisily. When she pulled the cup away, she had a dripping red mustache above her lip.

"It tastes so *bad*," she said to Tristan.

Tristan struggled to swallow a thick lump.

"Yuck. Totally gross."

It caught in his throat, and he choked it down.

"Is this enough? How much more do I have to drink?" he asked Mr. Moon.

"All of it," the teacher replied sternly. "Pretend you are drinking a milk shake."

"It doesn't taste like a milk shake," Ray groaned. "It tastes like spoiled tomato juice mixed with lumpy, sour buttermilk."

"The wolfbane herb is bitter," Mr. Moon said, watching them intently. "But the liquid is poison only to werewolves. The rest of you will be okay."

"Drink fast and it will be over," Angela chimed in.

"We'll never get the taste out of our mouths," Bella moaned.

Ray swallowed hard. "It felt like an eyeball!" he gasped. "Like I just swallowed an eyeball!"

Tristan choked down the last thick drops of liquid. Even after the cup was empty, he kept swallowing. Trying to swallow the sour taste away.

He turned and saw Rosa set her cup down. She wiped the red goo off her face with her hand.

Bella's whole body shook. She burped loudly. She grabbed her stomach. "I'm going to puke. Really."

Mr. Moon stepped toward her quickly. "You don't feel well? The wolfbane is starting to work on you?" His eyes flashed with excitement.

"That stuff would make *anyone* sick," Bella groaned. "Not just werewolves." Then she burped again.

Tristan took a deep breath. Then another.

Mr. Moon had his eyes on the clock. "Let's all count to twenty-five," he said. "By that time we will see who gets sick. And we will know if Tristan and Rosa are telling the truth."

"One . . . two . . . three . . ." Angela began to count.

Tristan stared hard at Rosa. She gripped the edge of the table with both hands. Her chin was trembling. Her eyes were wide with fright.

"Eighteen . . . nineteen . . ."

Angela didn't get to finish her count.

Rosa opened her mouth in a terrifying scream. She grabbed her stomach with both hands.

"It hurts! Ohh . . . it hurts!" she cried.

Tristan staggered back. He let out a sharp cry and grabbed his stomach.

He saw Bella and Ray staring at him in shock.

"Can't breathe . . ." he whispered. "Help me! Please help!"

He doubled over. "Ohhh, it hurts. It hurts! I can't breathe. Sick . . . I feel so sick."

Tristan and Rosa held their stomachs, groaning in pain.

"It's poison," Tristan whispered. "It really is poison."

"I . . . I don't believe it!" Ray cried.

"Tristan and Rosa were telling the truth!" Bella exclaimed. "They really are werewolves!"

Tristan dropped to his knees. He let out a whimper and hugged himself tightly.

Rosa's eyes rolled wildly in her head. "Poison . . ." she murmured weakly.

"Are you going to capture them?" Ray asked Mr. Moon. "Are you going to lock them in the cage?"

Mr. Moon shook his head. A thin smile crossed his face. "They're faking," he said.

Ray and Bella both uttered cries of surprise.

"Tristan and Rosa are faking," the teacher repeated. "They are not our werewolves."

Tristan dropped facedown on the floor. "Help me," he whispered. "Someone . . . help. I can't stand the . . . pain."

Rosa collapsed to the floor and rolled onto her back. "It hurts. . . . It hurts *so much!*"

"Get up. Both of you," Mr. Moon snapped.

"But they are in pain," Bella said. "Why do you say they are faking?"

"The wolfbane is a fake," Mr. Moon explained. "Angela made it last night."

"It's tomato juice and chocolate pudding and raisins and olives," Angela said.

"We don't have any wolfbane herb," Mr. Moon said. "I don't even know if wolfbane exists."

He reached down and tugged Tristan to his feet. "The drink tastes bad, but it isn't poison," he said. "Tristan and Rosa are faking."

Rosa angrily climbed to her feet. She glared at Mr. Moon.

"I knew what you and Tristan were trying to do," the teacher told her. "It was a lame idea. Did you really think I would let your friends go running for help?"

"We knew it wasn't real," Rosa said. "But we want to get out of here. Let us out!"

"No one can leave before midnight," Angela said. "No one can leave before we know who the *real* werewolf is."

She started to gather the goblets and place them back on the tray. "Almost midnight," she told her husband. "We will know the truth in a few minutes."

"Let me help you with the tray," Mr. Moon said. "I'd better prepare the cage for tonight's victim."

He picked up the tray and began to follow her to the kitchen.

"You'd better let us go—right now. We promised our parents we'd be home by eleven," Tristan called.

"They'll be worried," Rosa added. "They'll be over here any minute."

"Fine. Let them come," Mr. Moon replied. "It will be a total thrill for your parents to see us capture a real werewolf."

He and Angela disappeared into the kitchen.

Ray walked over and slapped Tristan on the back. "Nice try," he said. "I really believed you were poisoned. I really believed you and Rosa were werewolves."

"You fooled me, too," Bella said. "I mean, I know you're not werewolves. But when you started moaning and groaning like that . . ."

"It didn't work," Tristan said sadly. "Rosa and I thought he would keep us here and set you free. But it didn't work."

"Now what?" Rosa asked. "He's totally crazy. They both are. What are they going to do when the clock strikes twelve?"

"Maybe it will be okay," Ray said. "Maybe when they see that we aren't werewolves, they'll just let us go home."

Bella stared at Ray. "We're *not* werewolves, right? I mean, no one here is a werewolf?"

"Of course not," Ray replied.

Bella tugged tensely at her hair. "He . . . he's got me so mixed up. I don't know *what* to think."

Tristan let out a cry when the grandfather clock in the corner began to strike.

BONG . . . BONG . . . BONG . . .

"It's midnight," he gasped.

The four kids huddled close together, listening to the chimes of the clock.

BONG . . . BONG . . .

Tristan gazed out the front window. Like a big silver balloon, the full moon floated high in the night sky.

BONG . . . BONG . . . BONG . . .

Twelve chimes.

Twelve o'clock.

Midnight on Halloween night. A full-moon Halloween.

The hour of the wolf.

Now what? Tristan wondered, his eyes on the shimmering moon.

Now what?

The first scream from the kitchen made all four of them jump.

Tristan recognized Mr. Moon's terrified voice. *"Stop! Go away!"*

Angela's scream rang through the house. *"Don't touch me! Let go!"*

And then both of them were shrieking. Screaming at the top of their lungs.

"Help!"

"Help us!"

"Stop! Please! Don't!"

"Oh, help! Somebody—help us!"

"Stop! Please! Stop!"

"Ohhh—no!"

The cries of horror echoed from the kitchen.

Frozen in fear, Tristan heard a loud crash. The sound of breaking glass.

He heard a hard *thud*.

Mr. Moon uttered a sharp cry of pain.

"No! No! No!" Angela was screaming shrilly.

Another *thud*.

Then silence. A terrifying, still silence.

Tristan's whole body shuddered. Rosa grabbed his arm and squeezed it tightly without realizing it.

Ray and Bella had their mouths wide open in fear.

No one wanted to move.

"Wh-what is happening in there?" Ray stammered.

"Why are the Moons screaming like that?" Bella whispered.

It didn't take long to find out.

Tristan heard a high animal howl.

The rapid thud of footsteps.

Another howl.

And two snarling wolf creatures trotted into the room.

Their gray fur bristled on their backs. Their teeth were bared.

Glowing, dark eyes searched the room. Moving together, their paws pounded the floor heavily. Their long tails waved furiously behind them.

The wolves howled again.

"Werewolves!" Tristan cried.

"*No!* It can't be!" Bella shrieked.

Werewolves! Howling for us—howling in triumph, Tristan thought.

And as the raging creatures moved closer, trotting side by side, Tristan saw the blood on their claws.

And the chunks of skin clinging to their long, curled fangs.

Human skin?

What have they done to the Moons? Tristan wondered.

Did they *eat* them?

How did they get into the kitchen? Where did they come from?

"We—we're trapped!" Rosa gasped.

The wolf creatures lowered their heads as they moved toward the kids. They arched their backs, growling with each breath.

Preparing to attack.

Tristan and his friends backed to the wall.

The wolf creatures rose. Slashed the air with their blood-soaked claws.

And leaped.

Tristan dodged to the right.

The snarling wolf creature hit the wall.

Dazed, it let out a grunt and backed away, shaking its bristle-furred head.

The other werewolf sprang onto Ray. Ray dropped to the floor and spun away as the creature snapped its jaw inches from his head.

The first wolf creature leaped at Tristan again.

Tristan had no room to dodge. With a frightened cry, he threw his arms around the creature and tried to wrestle it to the floor.

"Help! Oh, help!" Bella was screaming at the top of her lungs, hands pressed to her cheeks.

Rosa stood stiffly, body tensed, ready to help

Tristan if he needed it.

Tristan struggled with the wolf creature. He dragged it to the floor and tried to roll on top of it.

But the creature was too strong. It quickly rolled over Tristan, opening its jagged-toothed jaw in a roar of victory. Then it lowered its head to attack.

Gasping for breath, Tristan raised his arms. Wrapped his hands around the creature's head.

He twisted the head one way, then the other. And tugged.

"Oh!" To Tristan's shock, the wolf head came off in his hands.

"Mr. Moon!" Tristan gasped.

The wolf head was a mask of rubber and fur. Mr. Moon grinned down at Tristan from inside the werewolf skin.

"Happy Halloween, everyone!" the teacher cried.

He climbed to his feet and helped pull Tristan up.

Beside him, Angela pulled off her wolf mask. Her face was pink and sweaty. Her blond hair was matted to her forehead.

"Surprise!" she cried breathlessly.

Mr. Moon tossed back his head and laughed. "You all look so terrified!" he exclaimed gleefully.

"You can relax now," Angela said. "Really."

Mr. Moon began to tug off the wolf skin. "This is a joke Angela and I play every Halloween," he said. "I picked you four kids to come to my party this year because you are my favorite students."

Tristan was still trembling from his wrestling match with Mr. Moon. He turned to Rosa.

She had her hands balled into fists. Her face was tight with anger. "You . . . you mean it's all a big joke?" she cried. "All of it?"

Mr. Moon and his wife nodded.

"It's all a big joke, except for one little thing," the teacher said. "Angela and I really are werewolves!"

Tristan's breath caught in his throat. He stared hard at the smiling teacher and his wife.

Mr. Moon and Angela burst out laughing.

"Only kidding," Mr. Moon said. "It's all a big joke. Really."

"We like to give kids a Halloween they won't forget," Angela said.

"And you won't forget this Halloween—will you, everyone?" Mr. Moon asked.

No one answered.

Tristan still felt too shocked to speak.

Finally, Ray broke the silence. "So . . . there are no werewolves? You don't really think that one of us is a werewolf?"

"No, we don't," Angela replied.

"It was all a joke," Mr. Moon said. "You don't really believe in werewolves—do you?"

"Does this mean we can leave?" Rosa asked.

Mr. Moon nodded. "Yes. Our party is over. You can all leave now."

"And don't worry. It isn't as late as we said it was," Angela said, straightening her hair with both hands. "It isn't midnight yet."

"I set all the clocks forward a bit," Mr. Moon explained. "So you could get home earlier. See?" He held up his watch. "It isn't midnight for another couple of minutes."

He walked over to the grandfather clock and reset it to the correct time.

"Oh, wow," Rosa sighed. "I don't believe it. I was so scared, but it was all a joke."

"I've never been so terrified in my life," Bella said, shaking her head.

"I hope you'll all forgive me," Mr. Moon said. "Angela and I throw these parties every year for my very special students. We just wanted to give you a few Halloween thrills."

Tristan started to the door. His legs still felt shaky, and his heart raced in his chest.

"So we can go now?" he asked.

Mr. Moon nodded. "Yes. Our party is over."

Angela hurried to block their way. "Stay and have

a glass of apple cider before you go," she said.

"No thanks," Rosa replied. "It's really late."

"My parents are going to be so angry that I wasn't home by eleven o'clock," Tristan said.

"Please tell them it was all my fault," Mr. Moon said.

They walked past the wolf skins piled on the floor as they made their way to the front door. Mr. Moon stepped up to the door and began to tug at the metal bolt.

He slapped his forehead. "Oh, wait. I forgot," he said. He turned to his wife. "Angela, push the button on the bookshelf. I forgot the doors are all bolted shut electronically."

Angela hurried to the bookshelf. She shoved aside some books.

Tristan could see the black control panel with its three red buttons.

Angela raised her hand and pressed the top button.

"Oh—no!" She let out a cry. Then she turned to them with the red button in her hand. "It . . . came off!"

Mr. Moon tugged at the heavy metal bolt. "Well, just put it back on," he said. "Put it back on and push it so these kids can go home."

Angela turned and struggled with the button. "It won't go," she said finally. "It won't go back on."

"Let me try it." Mr. Moon lumbered heavily across the room. He took the button from Angela and raised it to the control panel.

"There," he said finally. "I got the button back on."

He pushed it.

Once. Twice. Another time.

"It . . . it isn't working," he stammered. "The control seems to be broken."

"What does that mean?" Tristan asked, feeling a stab of panic tighten his chest. "How do we get out?"

"We can't," Mr. Moon replied. "We're trapped in here!"

"No! We've *got* to get home!" Tristan cried.

He grabbed the bolt handle with both hands and struggled to slide the bolt open.

It wouldn't budge.

"You've got to let us out of here!" Bella shouted in a trembling voice. "It's almost midnight and—"

BONG . . . BONG . . .

Tristan heard the big clock begin to chime again.

"Can you raise the bars?" Rosa asked. "We can all climb out a window."

"I'm pushing that button," Angela replied. "But it isn't working, either. I'm really sorry. Something has broken, I'm afraid."

BONG . . . BONG . . .

Tristan struggled with the front door. He tried twisting the knob and pulling the bolt at the same time.

"It won't work," Mr. Moon said. "It's all electronic, you see."

BONG . . . BONG . . .

"We can phone for help," Angela said. "I'm sure the phones are still working."

BONG . . .

"*Too late!*" Tristan growled. "*Too late for that now!*"

He could feel the change coming over him. The change he had felt on so many full-moon nights.

He could feel the pull of his skin, tightening over his bones.

His arms and legs began to itch as the stiff, dark fur poked up from his skin.

A low growl started deep in his chest and worked its way up through his throat—and out of his snout.

Changing. . . . Once again Tristan's body was changing.

The ears pointing up. The fur sprouting everywhere. The pointed teeth shooting out from his gums. Hot drool hitting the floor in front of him.

His body stooped now . . . stretching . . .

The skin stretching . . . the bones grinding as they changed his shape . . .

The color seeping from his eyes . . . He stared

at the black-and-white world. . . . Stared as an animal . . .

And felt the hunger.

The gnawing hunger that rumbled his belly.

The hunger that made him rage and roar.

And raise his hands—wolf paws now!—with the long claws curling out of them.

"OWOOOOOOOOOO!"

He turned and saw Rosa. Yes, Rosa, too.

Rosa the wolf creature. Scraping the air with her claws.

Thick gobs of white drool spilling over her fangs.

Roaring with the hunger, the same hunger Tristan felt.

Tristan turned and stared at Mr. Moon. The teacher had his arm around his wife. His eyes bulged, and he shook in terror and shock.

If only he had listened to us, Tristan thought.

Rosa and I confessed to him. We told him we were werewolves.

But he didn't believe us. Poor fool.

BONG . . . BONG.

The last two chimes of the clock.

Tristan turned to the window. The full moon so high in the sky now. So high it couldn't be seen from the window. From above the trees, its pale light washed in through the bars.

He and Rosa pawed the carpet. Then moved

toward Mr. Moon, Angela, Bella, and Ray.

"No—please!" Angela screamed. "Please—!"

"You . . . ignored the curfew!" Rosa growled.

"Our parents . . . they wanted us home by eleven," Tristan whispered. "They wanted us home so no one would see this!"

The four trembling victims backed up against the living room wall.

Tristan and Rosa moved closer, snapping their jaws, their long tongues licking their pointed fangs.

"But now you know the truth about us!" Rosa snarled.

"And now," Tristan growled, "we can't let any of you out alive!"

"Meat!" Rosa roared. "I'm soooo hungry!"

Tristan staggered forward. He raised his clawed wolf paws and prepared to attack.

His heart pounded so hard, he could hear the blood rushing through his veins. The excitement was always overwhelming on these nights.

The hunger . . . the animal feelings . . . the gnawing need to attack, to devour!

"Please!" Angela shrieked, covering her face with her hands. "Please—no!"

Tristan bent his legs, prepared to spring.

The loud chime of the front doorbell made him stop.

Tristan and Rosa both froze, hearts pounding,

jaws still snapping.

Another chime of the doorbell.

"Open up in there!" a stern voice shouted. "Police."

Tristan let out a gasp and sank back beside Rosa.

"Oh, thank goodness!" Mr. Moon cried. He darted past the two werewolves and ran to the front door.

"Thank goodness. Thank goodness you're here!" he shouted through the door.

"Open up," the officer ordered.

"I . . . I can't," Mr. Moon replied. "The bolt is stuck."

"We'll break it down," the officer replied.

A hard crash. The door shook.

Another hard crash. The bolt cracked off. The door swung open.

Two blue-uniformed police officers burst into the room, followed by Michael Moon. The officers were both tall and powerful-looking. One had long, curly red hair hanging from the back of his uniform cap.

"What's the story here?" he asked, his eyes moving around the room.

Michael ran over to his parents. "I escaped through the basement," he told them. "I had to bring the police. I couldn't let you do it again. I couldn't let you torture these kids with your horrible Halloween games."

"You—you don't understand!" Mr. Moon cried.

He turned and pointed at Tristan and Rosa with a trembling finger. "They—they're real!" he stammered.

"Yes!" Angela spoke up. "Those two. They're real werewolves!"

Tristan felt a stab of fear. He clamped his jaw shut. Ignoring his heaving chest, he backed alongside Rosa into the shadows.

"Capture them!" Mr. Moon screamed. "Hurry! Capture them! They're real werewolves! Capture them!"

The officers turned to look at Tristan and Rosa.

Tristan felt his fur bristle. He tensed his legs—and prepared to attack.

"Nice costumes," the red-haired officer said to Rosa and Tristan.

The two policemen turned back to the Moons.

"But they're not costumes!" Angela screamed. "Those two are *real* werewolves!"

"Mom—stop it," Michael said sharply. "I've already told these two policemen about your little problem. How you and Dad like to scare kids to death."

"No! Listen!" Mr. Moon screamed. "It's true this time! You've got to believe me!"

Both officers pulled out handcuffs. "Are you two going to come quietly?" one of them asked.

"No! Listen!" Mr. Moon shrieked.

"You're making a big mistake!" Angela cried. "We're not making it up! Those two are werewolves!"

"Yeah, sure. And I'm the son of Frankenstein!" the red-haired cop cracked. They slapped the cuffs onto the Moons.

Michael shook his head sadly. "I'm really sorry," he muttered to his parents. "But I had no choice. I couldn't let you do this again."

The cops turned back to Tristan and his friends. "Are you okay?"

All four of them nodded.

Tristan's heart pounded. The hunger gnawed at his belly. He wanted to toss back his head and howl. He wanted to sink his teeth into something soft and juicy.

I need food, he thought. I need *meat*—now!

His wolf body shook with the hunger. But he held himself back.

Michael Moon walked over to the four kids. "I'm sorry about my parents," he said. "But they're not well. They have mental problems."

"You're making a big mistake!" Mr. Moon shouted from across the room. "You are letting two werewolves get away!"

The officers dragged Mr. Moon and Angela to the door.

"My parents go from town to town, inviting kids to their totally scary Halloween parties. But they're too scary," Michael continued. "They keep kids trapped here. They make them eat disgusting things."

"That's really sad," Rosa whispered. A glob of drool ran down her snout. She quickly mopped it up with her furry paw.

"Every Halloween they throw a party just like this one," Michael said. "It's so sad. I—I don't know what will happen to us now."

"Yes. So sad," Tristan repeated. A growl of hunger shook his belly.

"But look at those two kids!" Angela cried. "They are wolves! They are really wolves!"

"Sorry," the red-haired cop said. "You've pulled this too many times."

He led the Moons to the door. "You'd better come too, son," he told Michael. "Will you kids be able to get home by yourselves okay?"

"No problem," Tristan growled.

"No—wait!" Bella cried, finally finding her voice. "Ray and I—we're not safe. We—"

Ray stared at Tristan and Rosa. "We need help!" he shouted.

Too late.

The door closed behind the Moons and the two cops.

Silence now.

Their faces wide with fright, Bella and Ray backed away from the two werewolves.

"The Moons *weren't* crazy!" Bella uttered. "They were right. You two *are* werewolves."

Ray raised his right hand as if swearing an oath. "But Bella and I won't tell anyone. We'll keep your secret. I promise."

The two of them were quaking with fear as Rosa and Tristan closed in on them.

"Let us go!" Bella pleaded. "We won't tell. We won't tell anyone. I swear!"

Tristan's stomach growled again. He licked his wet fangs.

"We're friends—right?" Ray said. "Friends?"

"You're right," Tristan snarled. "Friends. So get going. Hurry."

Ray swallowed hard. "Get going? You mean it?"

"Sure," Tristan said, his muscles tensed, legs ready to spring. "We're friends. So Rosa and I will be fair. Start running. We'll give you a ten-second head start!"

ABOUT THE AUTHOR

R.L. STINE says he has a great job. "My job is to give kids the CREEPS!" With his scary books, R.L. has terrified kids all over the world. He has sold over 300 million books, making him the best-selling children's author in history.

These days, R.L. is dishing out new frights in his series THE NIGHTMARE ROOM. When he isn't working, he likes to read old mysteries, watch *SpongeBob Squarepants* on TV, and take his dog, Nadine, for long walks around New York City, where he lives with his wife, Jane, and son, Matthew.

Take a look at what's ahead in
THE NIGHTMARE ROOM #11
Scare School

"AAAIIIEEE!"

I let out a scream and heaved my backpack against the wall.

Mom spun around from the kitchen sink. Dad jumped up from the breakfast table. "Sam, what is your problem?" he called.

"The stupid zipper is stuck again," I said.

I knew what was coming. Another lecture about holding my temper.

I counted to five under my breath. Mom was a little slow this morning. She usually starts the lecture by the count of three.

"Sam, you promised," she said, shaking her head.

"I know, I know," I muttered.

"You promised you would work on your temper," Dad said, walking over to me. Dad is very tall and broad like a middle linebacker. His friends all call him *Giant*.

I dragged the backpack up from the floor and tried the zipper again. "I said I would be careful not to lose my temper at my new school," I said.

"You wouldn't be starting at a new school if you

didn't get into so many fights at your old school," Mom said.

She gave me the hard stare. I call it the Evil Eye. It made her look like some kind of dangerous bird, like a hawk or a buzzard or something.

"Like I don't know that!" I snapped.

"Easy," Dad warned, raising one of his huge, beefy hands.

"I know, I know. I got kicked out of school, and you'll never forgive me," I said angrily. "But I didn't start that big shoving match. Really. It wasn't my fault."

Mom let out a long sigh. "Haven't we talked about blaming others for your problems, Sam? You had to leave your school because you were fighting. You can't blame anyone else for what you did."

"Yak, yak," I muttered. I finally got the stupid backpack zipper to move.

"Don't say 'yak yak' to your mother," Dad scolded.

"Sorry," I muttered. "Sorry, sorry, sorry."

Maybe I'll have that word tattooed on my forehead. Then I won't have to say it. I can just point.

Dad took a long sip from his coffee mug. He had his eyes narrowed on me. "Sam, I know you're tense about starting a new school."

I glanced at the clock. "Tense—and late," I said.

"Oh, my goodness!" Mom cried, spreading her hands over her cheeks. "We completely lost track of the time. Quick. Get your coat. I'll drive you."

A few seconds later, I was seated beside Mom in

the Taurus. I stared out at the gray November day. Most of the trees were already bare. The whole world appeared gray and washed-out.

The car roared as we rocketed down the narrow street. Mom drives like a NASCAR driver. The houses sped past in a blur. I pulled my seatbelt as tight as I could.

"A fresh new start," Mom said, trying to sound cheerful. She hadn't brushed her curly, red hair. It stuck out in all directions over the collar of her brown car coat.

"Mmm hmmm," I muttered.

I didn't want to say anything. I had my fingers crossed, praying that I could get out of the car without hearing another lecture.

"I know you're going to do really well at Broadmoor School," Mom said. She squealed to a stop halfway past a stoplight.

"Mmm hmmm." I kept my eyes out the window.

Suddenly, Mom reached out and squeezed my hand. "Be good, okay, Sam?"

Her sudden touch shocked me. We're not a real touchy-feely family. We're not constantly hugging each other the way families do on TV.

Once in a while, Dad will slap me a high five. That's about as far as we go.

I could see Mom was serious. And worried.

I swallowed hard. "I'll be different," I told her. "No problem."

She pulled the car to the curb. I stared out at my new school.

As I climbed out of the car, my chest suddenly felt kind of fluttery. My mouth was dry.

I really *am* nervous, I realized.

Of course, if I had known the terror that was waiting for me inside that building, I would have been a lot *more* nervous!

I would have turned and run and not looked back.

"Sam, your saxophone," Mom called from the car. "It's in the trunk— remember?"

"Oh. Right." I did forget.

She popped the trunk, and I pulled the big black sax case out.

I hope this school has a good band, I thought.

I've been taking sax lessons since I was barely as tall as the sax. I played in the jazz band at my old school. And some friends and I used to hang out and play in my garage.

Everyone says I'm really talented. I love to play. I love the idea of being able to make all that noise and make it really *rock*.

"Sam, what are you doing? Daydreaming? Don't just stand there. You're late," Mom called.

She squealed away from the curb. Made a U-turn onto someone's front lawn. Then headed back for home.

I balanced the backpack on my shoulders. Moved the sax case to my right hand. And stared at my new school.

What a gloomy sight.

My old school was brand new. It was modern and bright. And it had four separate buildings, and every building was painted a different bright color.

My old school was very outdoorsy, like those California schools on the TV shows. We walked to class outside. And there was a huge lawn with a little pond where everyone hung out and relaxed.

Broadmoor School wasn't like that.

It was a square-shaped, old building. Three stories tall with a flat, black roof. I guess it had been built of yellow brick. But most of the bricks had faded to brown.

On one wall of the building, the bricks were charred black. It looked as if a deep shadow hung over that wall. I guessed there had once been a fire there.

The grass in front of the building was patchy and choked with tall weeds. A barbed-wire fence ran around a small playground on the side. A U.S. flag snapped and flapped in the strong wind on top of a flagpole beside the entrance.

It doesn't look like a school, I thought. It looks like a prison!

I climbed the three steps and pulled open one of

the front doors. The door was heavy, hard to pull open. The glass in one of the windows was cracked.

I stepped into the front hall and waited for my eyes to adjust to the dim light. A long, dark hall stretched in front of me.

The walls were painted gray. Rows of black, metal lockers made them even darker. Only about half of the ceiling lights worked.

I took a few steps. The *thud* of my shoes rang out down the hall.

I glanced around, searching for the office.

Where is everyone? I thought.

Yes, I'm a few minutes late. But why isn't there anyone in the hall?

I'm assigned to Room 201, I reminded myself.

Is that on this floor? Or is it up one floor?

I began moving quickly down the hall, my eyes moving from side to side as I struggled to find a room number.

I passed a glass display case with one dust-covered basketball trophy. Above the case, a small blue-and-yellow banner read: GO, GOLDEN BEARS!

Two classrooms were dark and empty. I searched for room numbers but didn't see any.

Maybe they don't use this floor, I thought. Maybe all the classes are upstairs.

Lugging my sax case, I made my way down the long hall. The only sounds were the scrape of my shoes on the concrete floor and my shallow breathing.

The sax case began to feel heavier. I switched it to my other hand. Then I started walking again.

I turned a corner—and heard footsteps. Very light and rapid.

"Hey—!" I called out. "Is anyone there?"

My voice sounded hollow in the empty hall.

About three doorways down, I saw a flash of movement.

A figure darted out into the hall.

At first, I thought it was a little kid. He was only two or three feet high.

But then I realized he wasn't wearing any clothes.

He had his back to me. He didn't seem to know I was there.

His skin was greenish-yellow, covered in patches with green fur. He walked stooped over, on two legs.

His skinny arms stretched in front of him, nearly to the floor. He had small, pointed ears that stood straight up on a slender, bald head.

A giant green rat! I thought.

But then he stopped. And turned.

His mouth gaped open as he saw me.

He *hissed* at me. A frightening, angry sound like a snake about to attack.

And then he stepped into the light. And I saw him . . . saw him clearly.

And I cried out in shock and amazement.

The green, ratlike creature *had a HUMAN face*!